Shoreline of Infinity

Issue 6 Winter 2016/17

Science fiction magazine from Scotland

ISSN 2059-2590

Shoreline of Infinity is available in digital or print editions.

Submissions of fiction, art, reviews, poetry, non-fiction are welcomed:
visit the website to find out how to submit.

www.shorelineofinfinity.com

Publisher
The New Curiosity Shop
Edinburgh
Scotland

170117

Contents

Pull up a Log 3

Other Colours 5
Michael F Russell

Shaker Loop 21
Bo Balder

A Visit at St. Nick's 29
Gregg Chamberlain

Spaceman 33
Florence Vincent

Tales of the Beachcomber 41
Story - Mark Toner, Art Mark Toner and Tsu

Six 49
Hannah Lackoff

Goodnight New York, New York 61
Victoria Zelvin

The Descendant 69
Katy Lennon

The Worm 79
Russell Jones

SF Caledonia 88
Monica Burns

Annals of the Twenty-Ninth Century 94
Andrew Blair
CHAPTER XVII.
Between Heaven and Earth.

Interview: Stephen Palmer 102

Noise and Sparks 3: Interlude 110
Ruth EJ Booth

Reviews 114

Multiverse 124
Russell Jones
Grahaeme Barrasford Young
J.S. Watts

Parabolic Puzzles 132
Paul Holmes

Cover: Reader in the Library of Dreams by Steve Pickering

Editorial Team
Editor & Editor-in-Chief:
Noel Chidwick

Art Director:
Mark Toner

Deputy Editor & Poetry Editor:
Russell Jones

Reviews Editor:
Iain Maloney

Assistant Editor & First Reader:
Monica Burns

Copy editors: Iain Maloney,
Monica Burns, Russell Jones,
Rosie Gailor

Extra thanks to: Caroline
Grebbell , M Luke McDonell,
Chris Kelso

First Contact
www.shorelineofinfinity.com
contact@shorelineofInfinity.com
Twitter: @shoreinf
and on Facebook

Pull up a Log

Gareth L Powell posted this tweet on the day of the US Presidential election:

If you are that writer in 2056 reading this, please borrow your inventor friend's time-machine to nip back to us and hand us a copy of your book for review. It's no use in this timeline now, but it would be good to read what might have been...

While you're here, writer from the future, I hope you enjoy this Christmas flavoured issue. I like to imagine you returning to your present (hope the radiation levels are normalising), and sharing these wond'rous tales, pictures, poems, reviews, and writings with your friends.

You will also meet our new cover character—Reader. Stephen Pickering leapt at the brief of creating our covers for the coming year and we are delighted with the result.

On another note, a reader contacted us in the summer to say she would love to visit Shoreline HQ, and take a tour—we oblige in our seasonal comic story, and I hope, dear reader, it is as you imagined it would be.

Happy reading everyone!

Noel Chidwick
Editor-in-chief
Shoreline of Infinity
December 2016

Other Colours

Michael F Russell

Art: Mark Toner

H*e's close now. He can feel it. Everyone else has gone home: it is just himself left, staying late.*
Too late.
He is close now. Too close to share the moment with anyone else.

Sitting at his terminal, alone among banks of darkened workstations, Dr John Fisher studies the latest beam-collision signatures. He could do with a shave, a haircut and an ironed shirt; the glass of mulled wine he was offered sits beyond arms-length, unsipped. With thumb and slender forefinger he flips and tweaks the latest on-screen collider schematic, a femtosecond monochrome spray of sub-proton debris, fragmenting from a central collision point.

"Non-scalar," he mutters to himself. "Spin zero. But the electroweak breaking is not spontaneous." He frowns at the screen, whispering. "What is controlling it?"

Fisher cannot hear a breath being taken, and held.

He prods the screen. Nothing happens. The schematic, so easily manipulated, so pliable just a few seconds before, is unresponsive. He jabs at the screen a few more times and sits back, exasperated. Getting the tech-guys to fix it would be impossible at this time of year and he couldn't just pull the plug on the display, not on these machines, because it might affect the whole network.

He looks at his watch. The time is 11.17. Wrong date; too late. It takes him a moment to realize that the second hand has stopped. He takes out his mobile phone. It's the same: 11.17.

He waits. And waits.

11.17 it stays.

In his peripheral vision Fisher sees a man, standing, just a few metres away.

He gasps.

"What…Jesus, who the hell are you?"

The stranger is tall, in his 60s, his bearing is erect and motionless; face impassive, dark three-piece suit immaculate.

"I don't have a name," says the man calmly, a smile in his eyes, "but you can call me…Edward. I believe your grandfather had a friend by that name, a travelling magician, and you remember him fondly. I am his age and build, and I even sound like him. I'm Edward."

"You're not on the team," states Fisher. "How did you get past security, the scanners? How do you know all that about me?"

"No, I am not on the team, Dr Fisher."

Fisher looks uncertain. He waits, scratches his dark stubble.

"OK," he says, picking up the landline. "Let's find out who you are, how about that, um, Edward?"

There's no dialling tone. The line is dead. He'd been shown how to act calm with an intruder, what to do—how *not* to become agitated. But an afternoon's training is no preparation for the real thing. He slams the phone down and jumps away from the desk.

"Your research, Dr Fisher."

Fisher holds up his hands.

"Whoever you are, you have to leave. You shouldn't be in here." He stops. "What about my research?"

"It has provoked…strong interest."

Suddenly, Fisher thinks he understands.

"Look, if you're from the Tevatron Institute, I've told them that I'm not interested in a new position right now. It's a very generous offer they've made but…"

Edward shakes his head.

"Pan-dimensional entities, Dr Fisher. I am their conduit, their means of communication. These entities appreciate the effort you have expended, and they applaud your ingenuity…"

Pretending to take Edward seriously, Fisher edges away, nodding. It all sounds reasonable. Staying calm is very important with people like this. There's nothing, outwardly, to be alarmed about. It's all nice and calm and reasonable. That's the best way, surely, of dealing with people who are being unreasonable. Don't give them what they want. Don't get angry.

Ignoring what he'd been taught for the second time, Fisher springs forward, away from Edward and sprints past the banks of black-screened workstations towards the lab door. He slams the big red alarm button, but there's no klaxon, no flashing lights. He hits it again, pulls at a door that won't open. He heaves at it a few times, peers through the glass partition that separates the lab from a side office. There's no one around to help. But there is a connecting door on the far-side of the next room...

He picks up a chair, holds it out, legs forward, keeping Edward at bay. But Edward has not moved an inch.

"Really, Dr Fisher, there is no need for this."

"Please let me go."

Edward stiffens.

"Not yet."

"What do you want?"

"To talk."

Maybe that's fine. Maybe he's harmless. Easy enough just to hear him out. There's no problem with that.

Let the man speak.

Fisher throws the chair at the side office window. It smashes through, clatteringglassshattering onto the hard floor, tinkling into silence.

Silence.

And then the chair comes back through the window, its trajectory reversing. It flies towards Fisher and before he knows what's happening he's holding it again. The window unbreaks. It becomes whole.

Whimpering, Fisher drops the chair as if it had burned his hands. He stares at it, at the unbroken window, hardly able to comprehend what has just taken place. Calmly, Edward walks over and sets the steel-legged plastic chair the right way up.

"It is 11.17 and 23 seconds, Dr Fisher. It will stay that time until we have finished our conversation. I suggest you accept the situation and tailor you responses accordingly."

Fisher is quiet now. He has difficulty swallowing, standing. His legs are suddenly weak.

"What...what do you want from me?"

"It is very simple. You must—you will—discontinue your work, with immediate effect."

"My work? My...work?"

Edward slides the chair back under its desk.

"Blundering across the dimensional planes is extremely dangerous. You may call the entities I represent a police force, employed to correct any dangerous behaviour."

Now that his work has been threatened, Fisher rallies.

"Get out of here. I don't care who you represent, or how you...just get out. Nothing is going to get in the way of my work. Nothing and no-one."

Edward smiles.

"I'm afraid I cannot leave, not yet. The guardians will stop your research, Dr Fisher, one way or another. However, if you force them to materially intervene in this timeline, the consequences for the world you are familiar with could be severe."

Stopping work. Chairs flying backwards. Time reversing. Time stopping. Work stopping.

Fisher's eyes widen.

"I can't do that. I can't stop." Confused, he remembers the chair and the window that repaired itself. "It's all a trick, I don't know how...a trick."

Without warning, Edward steps smartly across the floor. Fisher backs away.

"Stand still," commands Edward. They are only two feet apart. Terrified, Fisher's back is against the lab door. Now he can see the man's smooth, pink cheeks, how neat his grey hair is, and the green light dancing in his eyes.

A wind blows out of nowhere.

Then they are outside, in bright daylight, on a lush green hillside, the air fresh and slightly damp, heavy with pollen and the scent of the sun on the ground...such purity in his lungs. And the forests rolling away beneath and around the hill, sunlight on a broad, silver river. Long grass waving in the breeze. Blue sky. Droning insects. Birds circling high above, black specks against the scudding white clouds.

Overcome, Fisher runs away from Edward, half blind in the dazzling daylight. He stumbles to his knees, his hands in the grass, gasping scratching clawing at the ground, at the grass, down to the dark soil, dirt on the ends of his fingers, under his fingernails. Impossible sensations overwhelm him, and his mind strains to hold back the flood. On his knees, he smells the earth on his hands and feels the sun on his face.

After a while he stops. The storm in his head subsides. Gentler, calmer now, breathing easier, he reaches out to a plant with huge yellow flowers, examines it for a moment. Drawing in the undefiled air he stands, absorbing a land that is unmarked by road or house or by any human structure. He understands what has happened, even if the how and why eludes him.

"When are we?" he shouts back. "When?"

Edward walks over.

"You tell me. Paleobiology formed part of your undergraduate studies."

Down on his knees again, Fisher has another look at the plant leaves, runs his finger down the thick, bristly stem.

"Quaternary period, definitely. I would say late Pleistocene, about 200,000 years BP. This is amazing. What I could do here. To bring proof back...so many gaps in our knowledge filled..."

Edward nods, his eyes glinting.

"This is the past, certainly. But a little later than you think. This is the year 1981."

Confused, Fisher stands, surveys the rolling countryside that surrounds him.

There's something about the river, something familiar. Fisher scans the horizon, squinting in the bright sun, casting a glance up at the circling birds. Down the wide-open sward an animal appears, bounding through the long grass and down to the river. Some kind of otter, but far bigger than any he'd ever seen before.

"How? What happened?"

"In this timeline...a change, many millions of years ago," replies Edward. "A certain small early mammal usurped the habitat of a certain other small early mammal. Subsequent speciation was affected. The change proliferated. And this world is the result."

Edward considers the river, darkening under sudden cloud-shadow. The breeze gusts through the long grass, fades to a restless whisper.

"Don't you know it, this place?"

Fisher isn't sure.

"In your timeline, this is Shooter's Hill." Edward points. "The Thames. Blackheath. Greenwich. No one will ever say these names, because Homo Sapiens do not evolve in this timeline." He pauses. "Homo Habilis, or a rough equivalent, is as clever as anything gets around here."

Out over the river one of the lazy birds is circling. It has spiralled downwards and Fisher can now see how big it is. The bird corkscrews round and round, down and down, then comes swooping, kiting from above the river, its huge shadow flashing across the grass, claws outstretched, sail-wings open, beaked red mouth agape, screeching.

Coming straight for him.

Just as Fisher screams, Edward appears in front of him. His glittering green eyes are the only constant as the world and the giant bird dissolve in a sudden gust of wind.

Face to face, they are back in the silent lab, where nothing moves— except Fisher, who bolts over to the door and pulls it, kicks it, desperate to escape. Clawing again. Frantic.

"It wasn't hunting you, Dr Fisher. You did not exist in that timeline."

"I don't give a fuck where I exist, I want out of here."

Motionless, Edward stands and waits until Fisher's tantrum runs out of steam. Eventually the struggle with the door ends and Fisher rests his head on the small pane of reinforced glass, cool against his skin.

There must be a way out of this. There has to be something he can do. Maybe he can kill Edward, destroy him, and the pan-dimensional entities will just...go away.

"Will that happen?" Fisher asks, without turning round. "If I continue my work, will I affect the future like that?"

"It's impossible to say. And that's exactly why the guardians won't allow it. Other species have been where you are now, and they took heed of the warning. Dimensional planes cannot be ruptured." Edward's tone hardens. "They cannot simply be broken into with this," he gestures at the frozen on-screen display," crude attempt at picking the lock." His demeanour softens, and the sly smile returns. His voice is smooth and evenly modulated once more. "Anything is possible, but the guardians like to keep a certain order. If everything happened at once then nothing could exist."

Fisher feels his resolve weaken. He turns around, glances at the screen he'd been studying, interrogating, pouring every ounce of himself into. This had been his life for almost six years. This is what he saw when he closed his eyes at night and when he opened them again just a few hours later. This is the course that nothing or no one must deflect, or endanger, not even his own family. His dreams of collisions and their consequences were in black and white. They were clearly defined as obsession or failure. And they were all he had.

"You praised my effort, my ingenuity."

"I did."

"The ingenuity that led me to this point, this discovery. But you want me to stop. You want me to turn my eyes away, just when the biggest secret of all is waiting." He points at the screen, a familiar anger building in him. "Right there. What do I do now if I stop all that—take up gardening? I can't be held responsible for the past, Edward, or whatever the hell your name is."

Green irises twinkle.

"Not even at any point in the 36 years 5 months and 14 days you have been alive? Are you responsible for nothing that has happened in that time?"

Fisher shakes his head, a weed of guilt uprooted.

"That's not what I meant, I meant big changes. World shattering events. I have no responsibility for those, not even in the time I've been alive."

"World shattering," repeats Edward. He walks over, fixing Fisher with his penetrating gaze. The eyes…where illumination and secret amusement dance. Face to face. Mind to mind.

And then: heat, like an oven door opening. A dark land. And snow, drifting down. Except it isn't snow. It is soot.

Before them, stretching away to a formless edge, is a smouldering blackened landscape. The ground is littered, carpeted, with pieces of charcoal no bigger than a fist, some of them still glowing orange, curls of smoke rising. From high ground, Fisher can see no plants or buildings or any living creatures, just carbonised rubble. Directly overhead, though the sun burns down, the stars are visible. Only at the far horizon is there any sky left, a strip of misty milk against the black.

This place is a great death. The song of life had been muted to stillness here. Silence had condensed to a singularity from which nothing of life could emerge. Fisher can feel it, the absence and the desolation. It chokes, assaults him, and he can barely speak.

"Earth? War?" He croaks, trying to swallow. "Asteroid?"

"War, yes, but on a much grander scale than you envisage. This is indeed the earth. Eight days ago it was a junior member in an alliance of galactic civilisations. Now it is no more.

"From the smallest microbe to the Great Barrier Reef, nothing lives here, in this timeline. Most of the atmosphere has been stripped, except for the heaviest elements, and the planet's axial tilt has been changed. You would not be able to breathe here. It is a dead world."

"Did I cause this?"

The way the land curves, the sides of that ravine in the middle distance...

"This also is 1981, Dr Fisher. Shooter's Hill."

Fisher gasps.

"A discovery is made in the year 1168 by a man who died as a child in your timeline. In your timeline, that discovery takes another 500 years, but here the process of technological change accelerates. By 1981 your species has travelled 30 light years in all directions. They make friends, and they make enemies."

Swallowing hard, Fisher's throat is as dry as the cauterised world around him. He kicks the rubble-cinders, and they give a dry metallic clink.

"Fucking toast," he whispers.

He turns to Edward, turns and wants to say something, but the urge to resist, the desire to project his own authority, is crumbling. Inviolable limits are being set, and, for once, he is powerless to change the terms of the debate. But his selfishness, the habit of getting his own way, isn't ready to lie down just yet.

"To be capable of travelling 30 light years, someone, in this timeline, must have copied my work, found out what I did."

"Of course. And she stopped, just like you are going to."

"Why? Did research like mine cause this?"

"No."

"Then why should..."

For the first time, Edward's serene façade cracks into anger. "Because all timelines are at risk." As he glares at Fisher, face to face, they are transported back to the lab. "This, all this destruction, is as nothing compared with the damage you could do, everywhen and everywhere. You have seen what effect even a slight change in the distant past can produce. Smashing your brutish way through the dimensional planes..." He waves the thought away; it is too fanciful to even formulate. "You will stop your work, Dr Fisher, or you will be stopped. You have no choice in the matter. I know that's an unusual situation for you, but there we are."

He falls silent, sits down heavily on a lab stool. Rubbing his face, Edward appears human, like a real person, one who loses his temper and then regrets it.

The smell of planetary incineration lingers. Fisher tastes it in his throat. He's at the lab's only window, staring blank-eyed at the outside world.

"It's not easy, when you have an important job to do," says Edward."
His voice pleads, but his eyes have the same hint of smile. Fisher, his
face pressed against the window stares outside. Caught in the glare of
car-park floodlights, there's an owl, frozen in fixed-wing flight, about
20 feet above the tarmac. The time is still 11.17 and 23 seconds.

"Others don't really understand," continues Edward, standing up.
"They don't appreciate the goals we set ourselves, or the pressure such
responsibility brings."

He places a hand over his heart. "Believe me. I know. I have
responsibilities, in every timeline."

Edward sighs.

"What's a man to do...time passes, and then you forget how to
smile. Worst of all it doesn't seem that important anymore." He goes
over to Fisher, who turns away from the window and is eased into
another time and place. "For some of us, there is only work and a
world of no colour. We only have the memory of another way of
existing, echoes of ordinary joy, of other people. It's the price we pay.
But it is a pity, don't you think?"

Fisher looks away from Edward's eyes, confused, anxious, as he
realises where he is.

"Simone!"

His soon-to-be ex-wife is sitting at a table, in a darkened room. The
TV is on, the sound turned low on a seasonal cookery programme. A
small angle-poise lamp glows next to her on the table, a glass of wine
by its side. In the corner of the living room a Christmas tree's red and
green lights wink and its tinsel glitters.

"This isn't 1981."

"No," says Edward. "This is tonight, three hours ago."

Simone is wrapping presents.

Taking sips from her drink, she wipes her nose and sweeps her long
unruly hair back, but it keeps falling over her face. In the dim light,
she looks even thinner than Fisher remembers. She bites a piece of
sellotape from its roll, almost snarling it off, and sticks the edges of the
wrapping paper down, then writes a name on a shop-bought sticker.
There are now four small presents on the table, each one wrapped in
Christmas paper. A bottle of after-shave will make a fifth. It's probably
for her dad. She is used to crying because it has become a chronic

condition. She can perform complex tasks even as the tears trickle down. Crying hardly gets in the way of anything anymore, although mixed with anger the cocktail can still overpower. Unnerved, Fisher starts pacing the room.

"She can't see or hear me, is that right?"

"Correct."

Edward observes, a dark suit hidden in shadow, the supreme persuader at work. Fisher looks around at the room he used to sit in, less and less often as the time went on and then not at all as their communal sourness drove him out. He sighs, annoyed.

"What are we doing here? Why is she crying?"

Edward gives a soft laugh.

"Really, Dr Fisher, an intelligent man like you."

"It is her who's divorcing me. You probably know that."

"Of course. I also know that your ex-wife is aware how important your work is to you, even now. That was never the issue. How important your family was to you—that was the question she asked—not directly, but in her own way. You did not answer that question because you understood nothing. But conscious choices often produce uncontrollable and unpleasant consequences." The smile in his eyes sharpens. "I think you're beginning to understand."

The room door opens. A small figure stands on the threshold, rubbing its eyes.

"Mum, I can't sleep. Is daddy here?"

Fisher reaches out to the boy, steps towards him.

"Sam!"

The boy shuffles into the room. Half asleep, wearing Spider-Man pyjamas. His mother quickly hides the Christmas presents under a newspaper, goes over to pick him up, wiping her eyes and scooping Sam into her arms.

"You've had a bad dream. It's not real. It's OK baby." She carries him out of the room and back to bed, leaving Fisher, as was so often the case, standing mute and seething in his own living room. But this time there is sadness, greater even than the one he felt on the dead earth.

"Here is the earth-shattering event you wanted, Dr Fisher. Her world has been broken apart, and that of your son. Sam doesn't sleep very well now; he's getting into trouble at school and your ex-wife is exhausted. I'm afraid you are responsible for this. It was your choice. She still loves you, but her heart is hardening, and soon it will be too late. In three weeks time your divorce will become absolute. Seventy-eight days from then your ex-wife meets someone else, through a work colleague—a tentative first date follows. It leads to a second date, and to a relationship." Edward waits.

"Selfishness is the bloom that chokes the garden. This other man has the capacity to put other people before himself."

Simone comes back in and takes a gulp of wine from her glass. She places the wrapped presents in a carrier bag, sniffing mechanically while wiping her eyes. Then she raises her head, seems to look directly at Fisher, as if she can see him. She looks into his eyes. Face to face.

"I did love her," says Fisher, tears in his eyes. "I do. I….don't know... don't...what to say."

As he reaches out, stricken, his ex-wife's face merges with the on-screen collision signature in the lab. He touches the monitor, a tear rolling down his cheeks. Edward is standing next to him. He speaks quietly.

"Existence is a web of complexity. Move too suddenly, too aggressively, and all you'll do is break threads. In higher dimensions there are other worlds, other realities. Other colours. Can you imagine a new colour? An entirely different colour to any you have ever seen?"

Fisher frowns. In a daze, he shakes his head, his fingers touching his screen wife, the wreckage of a violent event. There is no colour or shading in his life. All complexity had been reduced to black and white and his only focus was on destruction, on breaking down reality into perishable units of one that can never be truly isolated, for nothing exists alone. Atoms must always combine.

The illusion of being in control vanished. He was a child who dreamed he was a man. The course that could not be deflected or endangered was a dead end. There was no choice but to accept that, and turn around, to whatever wrecked paradise he'd abandoned.

Edward puts a hand gently on his shoulder.

"When you are ready—if that is ever the case—your species will be shown how to operate across the dimensional planes, but you will not be allowed to force your way in like children. There are always rules, and there are those who enforce them, usually to the benefit of those trying to break them."

He stops. He regards, for a moment.

"But you want to know. You are curious. And you want to leave your mark."

Fisher cannot hear the world exhaling, breathing again.

Sitting straight-backed at the terminal Edward types for 10 seconds, impossibly fast on the keyboard, his fingers a blur, streams of symbols and equations spreading across and down the screen. He stops typing when two-and-a-half pages have been filled.

The cursor blinks.

"Look elsewhere," he says. "It will be more productive, for yourself and for humanity, and safer."

Edward stands, straightens his perfect white cuffs, quiet and composed. He smiles, nods once, and disappears.

For a while Fisher can hardly move. He stares into space. Gradually, he refocuses, checks his watch, as if waking from a dream. The time is 11.21pm. The second hand ticks.

A sound at the window. A fluttering of wings. The owl he saw flying over the car-park has perched on the outside ledge, its huge dark eyes watching, blinking.

Fisher wipes his eyes and grabs the glass of cold mulled wine. He downs it in three gulps and sits to examine the first page of what Edward has typed. As he does so he picks up the phone, hesitates.

It might be too late to call her.

Too late.

Michael F Russell's first novel *Lie of the Land* was short-listed for last year's Saltire Society First Book of the Year award. He is deputy editor of the *West Highland Free Press* newspaper and his short fiction has appeared in *Gutter* and *Northwords Now*. His second novel, *Heliopause*, is looking for a home, and he is currently working on a third.

Illustrated by Sydney Jordan

Classic time travel stories from the last four decades gathered together in print for the very first time in this special edition

Published by Shoreline of Infinity Publications
paperback £10
also in ebook formats
available in all good bookshops or from

www.shorelineofinfinity.com

Shaker Loop

Bo Balder

Dad was demonstrating the disappearing drawers again. Patrick clung to his father's calf through the thick whipcord pants. A mist of one part irritation and two parts wonder descended on Patrick's uncles. Their stirring was a scary thing because their huge feet shuffled restlessly and asses got scratched, huge hands swinging down right past his face.

"Do it again, Paddy," his uncle Joe said.

"I got no keys to spare anymore," his dad said. "Anyone? Just gimme a matchbox or a cigarette, your keys are gonna be gone. Unless you don't believe me, of course."

"A waste of a good smoke," Uncle Riley said. His fingers, fidgeting with a freshly rolled cigarette, hung down next to Patrick's nose. His mom had recently issued a ban on smoking indoors. It didn't make the Christmas gathering any mellower.

"No one?" his dad said. "Joyce? Bring me a fork or something?"

"What? You want the good silver to disappear?" his mom yelled back.

"Here," Patrick said. He held out his prize possession, a purple and green Leatherhead figure from Teenage Mutant Ninja Turtles. If something made the keys disappear, he figured Leatherhead would know what to do with it. Anyway, he wasn't willing to risk Donatello or Leonardo.

"Hey, thanks, kid," dad said.

He held the figurine up for all the uncles to see.

Dad put Leatherhead in the left drawer. Not that it mattered, loose change and spare rubber bands disappeared from the right drawer just the same.

"You guys, look carefully. One toy. Everybody happy it's in there?"

"Yeah, yeah," Uncle Rod said. "You missed your calling, Pads, you should have joined the carnival after all."

Dad shoved the drawer shut with more force than necessary."Okay, I'm gonna step back now. Roddy, you wanna do the honors?"

"What?" Uncle Joe said. "You just skip over your little brother? Nice going."

Patrick shoved his head against his dad's thighs. Not again. They had such loud voices, and with their big bellies and big hands they made the house seem so small. If it hadn't been snowing he'd have been in the treehouse looking over the lake. He was just like mom, or so dad said. Shy, bookish. Patrick wasn't sure that he was, he just didn't like his uncles always shouting and arguing and getting red in the face as the evening progressed.

"Hey!" Uncle Roddy said. "It's gone. How did you do that?"

He bent over and peered into the drawer, feeling inside it with his big hands. Patrick's dad intervened when Roddy threatened to yank the drawer from the casing.

"Hey, hey, careful, it's an heirloom."

"Doesn't mean it's yours," Uncle Roddy bit back. "You live here coz you're the eldest, but it's our house, too."

Uncle Joe intervened, as he always did. His father and uncles withdrew to the den to drink some more.

An heirloom. What did that mean? It was a shiny table from a kind of whirly wood. You couldn't play on it because there were no chairs allowed in the hall and anyway it was tiny. Grown-ups used it to put keys on or mail. But it did kind of get in the way of using the black-and-white tiles in the hallway for sliding. So all in all Patrick didn't think it was a very good piece of furniture. Maybe heirloom meant "kind of useless."

Patrick stood on tiptoes to check if Uncle Rod had been right. Yep, Leatherhead was gone. He opened the right drawer to check if the figurine was in there. All he found was a funny thing, like a tiny flat walkie-talkie. Only it was a gross, girly pink. And nothing happened if you pressed the buttons. He put it back. The right drawer only ever produced stuff like that, shiny, pretty, but pointless. If you put it back in, it disappeared.

His eyes prickled. Maybe he shouldn't have given Leatherhead away. He'd just wanted the uncles to stop wrangling. Mom was in the kitchen, grousing about making lunch for so many people. Better not to disturb her.

He went to his room to cuddle up with Leonardo and Donatello.

❋

When the last uncle had left, back to their normal lives, Patrick could breathe again. He climbed on the deep sills of the garden-side windows and closed the curtains behind him. It was dark outside, so he couldn't see anything, but it was safe and silent. No uncles to punch his arm or rough up his hair. The look on his dad's face meant he had to pretend to like that stuff, and that was the worst.

Mom yelled that dinner was ready. It would be warmed-up macaroni and cheese, his favorite. Dad took his plate outside to do some banging and swearing in the shed. He hung out with his brothers for the holiday duration and then he got mad he hadn't gotten around to fixing anything in grandpa's old workshop.

Patrick had proposed not inviting the uncles, but although mom had smiled at him, she'd also said they couldn't do that. "It's their house as much as ours, hon. We should be happy we get to live in it all the time."

Dad returned and played with the side table some more. Patrick didn't join him because he was tired of watching things disappear.

He slid off his chair to get in some reading time upstairs before Mom would make him turn off the light. Dad didn't want him to read during the day either, he should play outside like a little man.

As he crossed the hallway, dad grabbed his shoulder.

Patrick winced and tried to pull away. What had he done now?

But dad didn't box his ears or anything. He pulled him in against his oil and beer smelling shirt and mumbled something in his hair.

"What?" Patrick said.

"Nothing, buddy. Don't look so worried. You're my little guy, you know that, right?"

The only possible answer was yes.

Dad let him go. "Go read. It's fine."

Too surprised at this change of heart to answer, Patrick ran up the stairs to get to his book. He didn't want to waste any more good reading time.

Still reverberating from an unexpected divorce, Patrick returned to the lake house after his parents died. He just wanted to clear out some personal items and sell up the rest. Uncle Roddy and his family had dropped out of sight, and Patrick hadn't been able to locate his one cousin, Bee, Uncle Joe's daughter. The others had died before his dad.

He roamed through the emptying rooms as he triaged pieces for the bonfire or the yard sale, missing, strangely enough, the rowdy brothers and their fights. Six of them, full of vim and vigor, and now he was the only one of the next generation. And his own kids hadn't been allowed to come. His ex stuck to a rigid schedule of once a month, which the overly righteous judge had agreed to. He'd begged Allyson to lighten up just this once; they could see the old lake house, it had been in the family for generations…but no. No kids. Just him. Thirty-seven and counting.

He ran his hand over the old-fashioned wainscoting in the hallway. With his mother's rugs and knickknacks gone, it had regained some of its former grandeur. Those black and white tiles sure had been nice to glide on.

The Shaker sidetable was missing, like many of the old-looking pieces of furniture he remembered. His mother had never liked them – had she been selling them off over the years? Maybe it was in the shed.

The shed yielded up more burnable junk, but no sidetable. He wasn't sure why it mattered, he'd never thought about the thing in all those years.

He worked until late in the afternoon. The burnable pile was getting too high to toss more stuff on, but it seemed a waste of a good fire to light it by day. He loaded the sellable pieces into the truck. Driving through miles of bare trees, he rolled into the sleepy town, emptier than before, with more closed-up stores than he remembered. The antique cum junk cum loved-clothing store was still open.

Craig, the owner, still shock-haired although it had gone white, plucked his lower lip. "Some nice things in there, Paddy, but business isn't doing so great. Can't offer you much for it. How about a trade?"

Patrick laughed. "For what? I can't take stuff with me, I'm flying home after I sell this truck."

"I'll take the truck," Craig said. "Have a browse in my store. I'll give you more money's worth in trade than I can offer in cash."

God, that was sad. When he was a kid, it had felt like a happy, prosperous town, full of smiling people, so different from the grey frowns of Chicago townhouses.

"Okay," he said and followed Craig into the store.

And there it was. Amidst a jumble of incomplete china sets, stacked plastic chairs, football trophies, black and white TVs, art deco radio sets, mysterious chrome rods and other dusty, unappealing objects, stood the Shaker sidetable. Shinier, the wonky forepaw fixed with a pale synthetic, like a pony with a white fetlock. But it had somehow become prettier now, since Allyson had taught him about Shaker furniture in the intervening years.

"Where did you get that?"

"That's my white elephant. I keep having to buy it back because people complain about things disappearing and appearing in it." Craig looked as if he wished he'd kept his mouth shut.

"Huh. My parents used to own it, I think. Did my mom sell you this? "

"Before my time, I guess. You want it back? I'd be willing to include it in the trade," Craig said, a shade too eager.

Patrick scratched his head. Did he want the damn thing back? He didn't have any particularly important memories of it. He'd lost some kind of toy to it, which had sucked. Still.

He opened the left drawer.

And closed his hand possessively around Leatherhead. It couldn't be. But his hand knew it was the one he lost and didn't intend to let go. There was more in the drawer besides the figurine: a bunch of keys, a lighter, some change.

Patrick lifted the key label with his other hand. *3789 Wichita Rd.*, it said in his grandfather's shaky writing. It couldn't be. But here they were, all the objects that his dad and his uncles had tossed into the left drawer. He even smelled pine needles and rum. Christmas smells.

He put Leatherhead in his pocket, encountering something else in there. He fished it out. A broken cell phone from his daughter Hollis, forgotten in this ancient waxed coat, which he hardly ever used in the city.

He tossed it in the right drawer.

Right drawer goes back thirty years, left drawer goes forward thirty years, he mumbled to himself.

"You want it?" Craig asked.

Patrick startled. He'd forgotten all about the man and the stuff in his truck, the trade. But first he had to do something. Alone.

"Yeah," he said. "I do. You get started getting my stuff in here, I just need to do something."

Craig went.

He and his father had never seen eye to eye; he hadn't gone home more than once a year, if that, since college, and avoided talking to the old man as much as he could.

But the pain of separation from his own kids had made him wise to distant dads. They had feelings. Fathers did love, even if they sometimes couldn't show it much.

Patrick found a business card in his wallet, the one screaming in shonky purple characters: Associate Professor, Dept. Of English Literature, Northwestern.

"Dad, I love you," he wrote on the front. "From your son Patrick, December 2016."

He folded the scrap of paper, put it in the right drawer and shoved it shut before he could change his mind.

A Visit at St. Nick's

Gregg Chamberlain

"Is that so?" asked Santa Claus.

The little girl nodded. "Uh huh."

"A time traveller!" Santa exclaimed. "That's what you're going to be when you grow up?"

Another nod.

Santa chuckled. "Well, isn't that wonderful? Smile now."

He gestured, and together they turned to face the camera. There was a flash. The little girl's eyes blinked with the after-glare.

"Maybe we'll cross paths again during one of your trips," said Santa, still chuckling. "Time to go now."

He helped the little girl slide off his lap and into the waiting arms of a pretty, tall, young elf standing beside Santa's throne. She led the little girl by the hand over to where a harried-looking woman waited at the exit from Santa's Christmas Workshop in the crowded mall.

"Ready to go, Lizzy?" the woman asked. Already she was looking around the huge mall foyer, searching for her next destination and also the one after that.

The little girl nodded and took her mother's hand. The smiling elf held out a clipboard and a pen.

"Just mark whether you'd like prints or digitals," she said. "Also fill in either the email or the postal address line."

She watched as the woman's face scrunched up in thought, forehead wrinkling with stress lines. A single strand of silver hair showed among the brown. Still smiling, the elf reached out, placed a hand on the woman's shoulder, and gently squeezed.

"Hey," she said, as the woman looked up. "It's okay. You're doing fine." Her smile broadened. "You're a very good mother."

The woman blinked in confusion. Then smiled slowly in return. "Thanks," she said, and finished filling out the form.

After getting back her clipboard along with the advance payment from a debit card swipe, the elf watched the mother and daughter quickly vanish into the mall crowd. She returned to Santa's Christmas Workshop, taking up a position beside another girl, also dressed in elf costume. A third helper elf manned the camera while a fourth was stationed beside the throne waiting to escort yet another child away after his visit with Santa.

"How you doing, Kara?" she asked.

Her fellow elf groaned. "My feet hurt. My legs hurt. My back hurts. I think even my smile hurts. So looking forward to break time. Don't you just hate this Christmas Eve shift, Liz? It's like a freaking madhouse."

"Always is when everyone's in a rush to get things done," Elizabeth replied. "All those last-minute items we all have to check off our lists."

She looked back at the crowd, just in time to see little Lizzy's mother give her daughter a surprise hug. Elizabeth the Elf felt a warm, new memory slip suddenly into place. A sad smile appeared on her face.

"Especially if there's something important you need to do."

Gregg Chamberlain, a community newspaper reporter four decades in the trade, lives in Ontario, Canada, with his missus, Anne, and a clowder of four cats. Besides writing genre fiction, he crafts zombie filk and indulges in the Canadian tradition of puns on the unsuspecting.

Spaceman

Florence Vincent

I n a quiet bar towards the northern pole of a cold blue moon, the blind man sits and rubs his head, trying to remember where he left his eyes.

He should have known that it would come to this. That boarding the Exxtris for one last cruise was not a decision he should have made, not after what happened last time.

Like always he can remember, if not *how* and *when* he has come to be in the bar, at least *why*. The images loop in the front of his head with astonishing, painful clarity; he watches and despairs.

Here he is sucking the endocrinal fluid from the crested pajibet's spines (so very moreish) and doing impressions with his lower mandibles.

Here he is inhaling two cartons of Drunksteam and running slow circles on the ceiling of the arboretum.

Here he is licking the venom pads of the beautiful Blashphelt girl with the soft wet mouth and telling her about his trick with the eyes. That, thinking back, was his worst mistake.

What is it? he wonders, sliding hands and feet around him and finding a cold, polished counter, a damp carpet. What is it that makes him do these things? The room smells of alcohol, and of waste material and slightly of burning, though the heat sensors at the back of his head indicate a low, stable temperature. It seems to be a bar, though it is exceedingly quiet. As his sub-mind runs a location marker, picking up cues from his surroundings to determine where exactly he is, the blind man makes a list of promises to himself.

No more booze cruises through the galaxy. No more getting intoxicated and demanding to be dropped at the nearest bar. No more taking his eyes out to impress the ladies.

In fact, perhaps the drink he has here, at (the location marker chimes) *THE OLD BELL INN, GREAT ECCLESTON* will be his last. When it opens, that is, and someone comes to take his order.

One last drink here while he waits for the Exxtris to swoop back over and pick him up, lesson learned.

Yes, he nods to himself, this will definitely be the last time.

※

In the darkness the doctor drives home, pinching finger and thumb into the corners of his eyes to keep them open. The road in front is illuminated harshly, his headlights two bright nets catching hare, pheasant, and leaves knocked along by the night wind. He is caught between the desire to get home quickly and the fear he will clip something, his bonnet tossing the corpse out into the road ahead where it will die in the spotlight of his full beams. He has never enjoyed theatre.

The doctor feels his foot ease on the accelerator (decision made) and wonders what he would give to have someone go into his brain and slice out every death scene he has ever witnessed. Sometimes he thinks he would give an entire limb. Put him under general and let them cut it off and take it away in exchange for a fresh, clean mind. It wouldn't be so bad, living without an arm or a leg.

He switches on the radio and turns the knob, seeking Christmas music. He isn't cynical about these things, not like other men his age. Hearing these songs takes him back to Christmas mornings with his mother, with his own children. A smell of gravy, cloves, pine needles, yards of wrapping paper crinkling underfoot. Eventually he settles on one station playing that god-awful Chris de Burgh song that secretly, he has always loved. He sings along trying to focus on the lyrics, trying not to think about other things.

If he'd known Mrs Cooper was dying he wouldn't have taken the call. He would have rung for an ambulance and gone back to bed, nestled close to his wife and waited for Christmas morning. Instead he rose, made coffee and crept outside to the car, passing the dark Christmas tree in the hall (how gloomy it looked without the lights on). Driving out to the Cooper house in the dark, he walked in to find her lying on the kitchen floor in a puddle of urine, using the last air in her lungs to recite a recipe for lemon cake.

And now he pinches sleep from his eyes and heads home to his wife, who will wake as he comes into the bedroom and ask him – that switched-off, sleep-rumpled look in her eyes – if Mrs Cooper

is alright. And he will have to tell her, at three am on Christmas morning, the first she will be spending without her children, that the old woman is dead.

He can't face that. Not without a drink in him. Not without a moment to himself away from the liquid dark of this endless road. And like that, a fairy light blinks on somewhere in his brain. He feels his hand go to the indicator, his right foot move to the brake to slow and take the next turning, instead of following the road home. A few minutes later his headlights catch new prey: a sign, decked in holly for the season and reading *The Old Bell Inn, Food Served All Day*. Thank god for Susan and her spare key.

*

He should be the most interesting man in the galaxy. Not only because he's a traveller from the other side of the universe, but because of his species' impressive, frenzied appetite for survival. This is why, of course, he worries that if you stripped away the adaptations there would be nothing to him. That he would be small and boring and easily forgotten in the too-large universe.

The blind man is feeling glum and he needs a drink badly. So when there is a sound from across the room, a scraping like metal against metal, he brightens, thinking that perhaps the bar is finally opening. In the next moment he feels his defences go up, becomes aware of his sub-mind reading the air for signs of danger. An awareness flickers into life somewhere and he knows before he knows that he is about to come face to face with his first ever human.

Oh fuck, he thinks. I'm on fucking Earth.

※

The door is stiffer than the doctor expected and on the sixth try of the key he loses his nerve, which is – things being the way they are – the exact moment the lock gives. He stumbles forward and finds himself standing in the dark doorway of the pub.

He clears his throat, straightens his collar for no one in particular and makes for the bar. No going back now that he's inside. He will have his little whisky, leave a few coins on the bar and drive home. By that time, the image of Mrs Cooper might have faded just enough for him to sleep.

Of course, two steps from the bar his skin prickles and he realises he is not alone. There at the end, just visible in the dark, a man sits, hunching forward. The doctor freezes, straightens his collar again.

"I'm not breaking in," he says for some reason. "I'm a friend of Susan's."

The man says nothing, simply shifts on his bar stool a little. He seems an odd-looking fellow, something indistinct about him.

"I'm just having one, then heading home. Are you a friend of the family?"

The other man looks up then and smiles very broadly. The doctor is relieved. He's just an old drunk, an uncle or distant cousin visiting for the season. There seems a look of sadness about him, like he has lost something, which is perhaps why he has been left to his own devices down here while Susan and her husband sleep upstairs.

The doctor flicks on the lights behind the bar, pours his whisky and raises his glass in the direction of the drunk. He has found himself glad, in an unexpected way, that he isn't alone.

His shift adaptation kicked in. It must have, seeing how the human hasn't screamed yet. How long it will last, the blind man doesn't know. What will happen when the shift fails, he doesn't know. In a worst case scenario, the Exxtris turns up while the human is still here (what were they thinking, dropping him on Earth?). He tries to focus on finding a solution but all he can think of is how annoying it is that he shifted without even realising. How helpless he feels when his sub-mind does these things before even asking him.

The human is talking to him, in an annoying way, and the blind man wonders whether he should eat him, and wonders when the Exxtris will be back, and wonders where the fucking fuck his eyes are.

✳

In the toilet, the doctor pisses and smells espresso. The stench of un-metabolised coffee wafting from the hot stream turns his stomach, and makes him feel scared and alone all of a sudden. Mrs Cooper is dead and he has broken into a pub and is sitting with an old drunk who may well be brain-damaged. Why did he come here when he could have gone home to his wife? He thinks about how much he loves her, how when she lets him be the little spoon his buttocks fit so neatly into the warm nook of her lap that he forgets where he ends and she begins. If he had only followed the road straight, he could have been lying there with her now.

He zips up and washes his hands three times. Back at the bar he will throw down a ten-pound note and leave, and he will speed home to his wife's warm lap. They will spend Christmas together, open a bottle of good champagne, Skype the children in London and Beijing. Celebrate the fact that, after all these years, it's just the two of them again, more in love than ever. At bedtime, she might even lift her nightgown over her head, pull him towards her so they can lie naked together. Skin on skin, mouths locked, hands exploring one another's soft places with the shyness of teenagers. At the thought of that, he feels his penis tick to the side like a needle on a Geiger counter.

✳

In the bar the blind man is growing increasingly desperate. Desperate for a drink, desperate for a sign that he has not been left on Earth for good, blind and helpless, a slave to his own unconscious systems. Things being the way they are, of course, at the very moment he is about to get up and go out the door, something tingles at the back of his skull.

It's the familiar *bing bong* of the comms system, a message from the Exxtris. They're back to pick him up and yes – they have his eyes. They want to know if he has sobered up, learnt his lesson, if he'll pay for the damage done to the arboretum. The relief floods through him like a hit of Drunksteam. He messages them back (*YES YES YES!*) and clicks off.

He will change, he knows that now. He will stop drinking, stop showing off. Start having conversations with people about real, important issues like politics and religion, and whether or not it is ethically sound to breed crested pajibets in such a way that their engorged endocrinal sacs prevent them from walking. There it is; he will become a campaigner for insect rights. He will be noble, beloved of the common people.

But will it still be enough? What if he gets back on board the Exxtris to find – despite all their chiding – that they still expect the same old jester? What if he is not enough without a new show, a new impression to keep them entertained?

When the human comes back into the room, the blind man's conviction fails him. He has realised – half relieved, half disappointed – that the solution is right in front of him, or at least in the same room.

As the doctor walks to the bar, tapping the bells on the Christmas wreath, humming Chris de Burgh and pulling out a crisp ten-pound note, the blind man messages the Exxtris for a second time.

MAKE THAT TWO FOR TRANSPORT, reads the transmission. *I'VE GOT YOU ALL A PRESENT.*

Yes, he thinks. This will really wow them.

Florence Vincent was born in London in 1988. She has lived in Edinburgh on and off since 2010, when she moved to the city for a Creative Writing Masters. These days she spends her time working on her first novel, watching sci-fi box sets and compiling Chris de Burgh playlists.

TALES OF THE BEACHCOMBER
'TWAS THE DIMENSIONAL CROSS-RIP AT THE TURN OF THE YEAR
STORY - MARK TONER
ART - TONER AND TSU

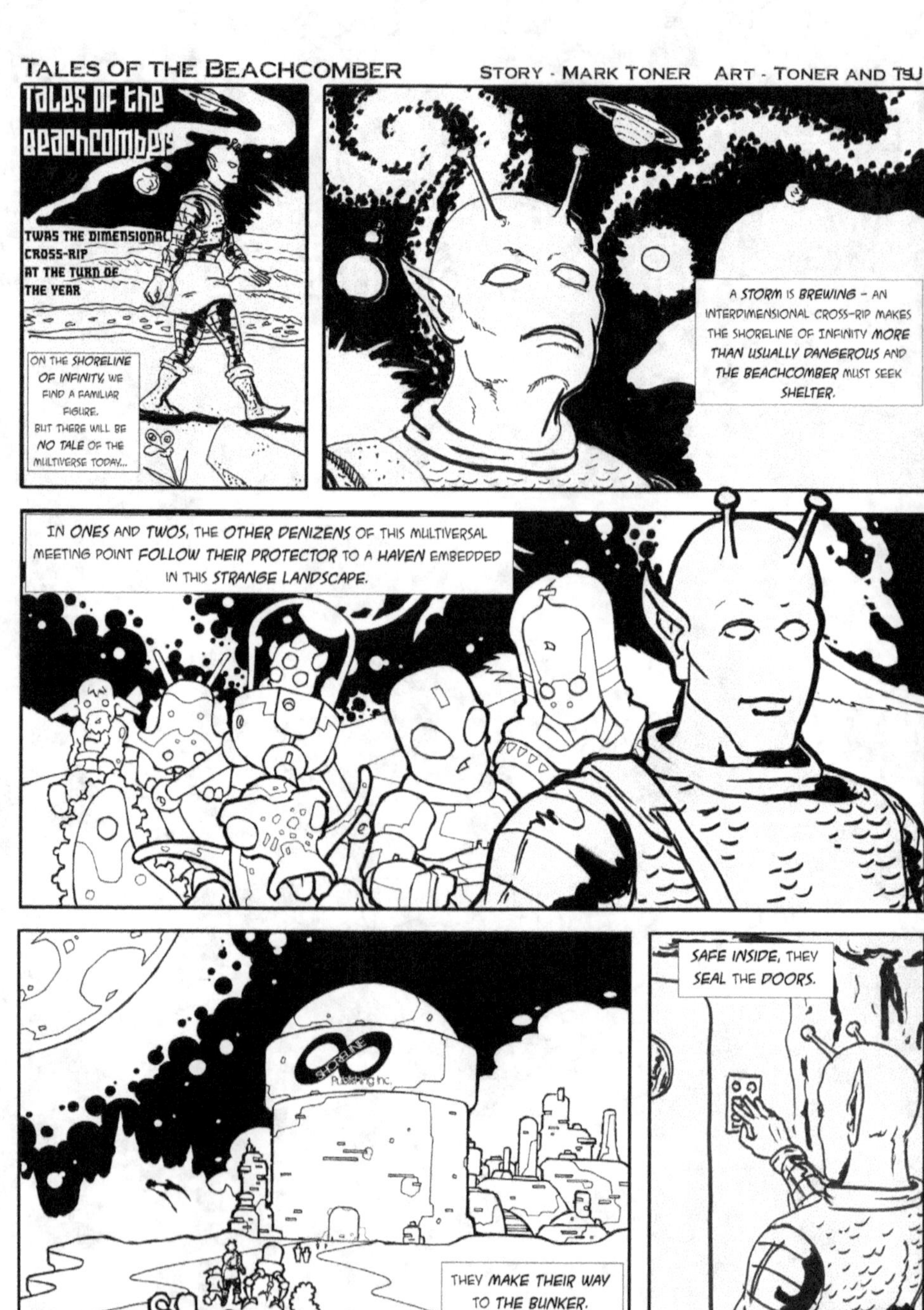

TALES OF THE BEACHCOMBER   STORY - MARK TONER   ART - TONER AND TSU

TALES OF THE BEACHCOMBER
TWAS THE DIMENSIONAL CROSS-RIP AT THE TURN OF THE YEAR
ON THE SHORELINE OF INFINITY, WE FIND A FAMILIAR FIGURE.
BUT THERE WILL BE NO TALE OF THE MULTIVERSE TODAY...

A STORM IS BREWING — AN INTERDIMENSIONAL CROSS-RIP MAKES THE SHORELINE OF INFINITY MORE THAN USUALLY DANGEROUS AND THE BEACHCOMBER MUST SEEK SHELTER.

IN ONES AND TWOS, THE OTHER DENIZENS OF THIS MULTIVERSAL MEETING POINT FOLLOW THEIR PROTECTOR TO A HAVEN EMBEDDED IN THIS STRANGE LANDSCAPE.

SHORELINE Publishing Inc.
THEY MAKE THEIR WAY TO THE BUNKER.

SAFE INSIDE, THEY SEAL THE DOORS.

"TWAS THE DIMENTIONAL CROSS-RIP AT THE TURN OF THE YEAR"
BUT LOOK! THERE IS ONE FOOLHARDY TRAVELLER RISKING THE BRANE CLASHING NIGHT.
HIS SHIP CAREENS THROUGH THE STORM ...
... SEEKING OUT THE BUNKER ON THE SHORELINE.
THE CRAZED PILOT LANDS HIS SHIP.
HE CRACKS THE SEAL AND OPENS THE DOOR FROM THE SAUCER PORT.

TALES OF THE BEACHCOMBER

STORY · MARK TONER   ART · TONER AND TSU

WHAT LIES WITHIN?
ZIG-ZAGGING ZELAZNY!

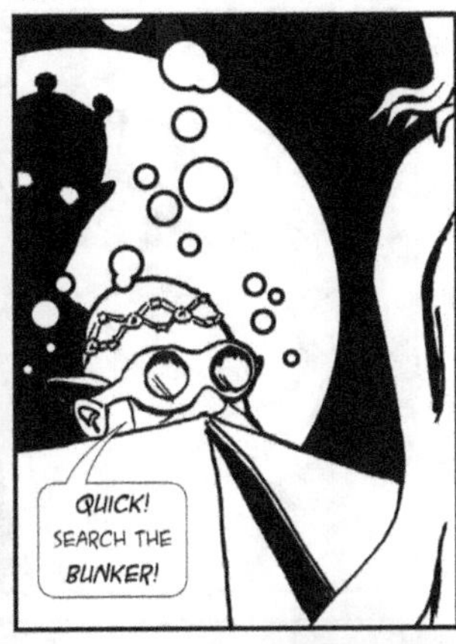
QUICK! SEARCH THE BUNKER!

A FRANTIC SEARCH ...
EDITO
STO
HOPP

... REVEALS ...

... MANY MISSING MAGAZINE MINIONS!
ART
PIT

THERE'S ONLY ONE THING TO DO - ...
THE CLEANERS - THE ONLY BEINGS ABLE TO PENETRATE ALL SIX DIMENSIONS OF THE SHORELINE BUNKER.
QX, CHIEF!
... ASSEMBLE THE CLEANING STAFF!

IN ODD INTERDIMENSIONAL CORNERS, THE CLEANERS SOON BEGIN TO FIND MORE PACKAGES.

MANY OF THE MISSING CREATURES ARE FOUND ...
... BUT NOT ALL.

THEN
WHO IS THAT?!

HE'S GOT A BUBBLE UNIVERSE SACK!

OUR MISSING PEOPLE - THEY MIGHT BE IN THERE!

GUIDED BY THE HIGHER DIMENSIONAL SENSES OF THE CLEANING STAFF, THEY GIVE CHASE!
HO!
HO!
HO!
DON'T LET HIM GET TO HIS SHIP!
SNIP!
EEK!
DON'T MESS WITH AN EDITOR!
HOORAY! THE MISSING PARCELS!
THERE WAS SOMETHING FAMILIAR BUT OPPOSITE ABOUT THAT STRANGER.
SEASONS GREETINGS, SHORELINERS!

Wallace
West

Six

Hannah Lackoff

Art: Wallace West

Sun up on the island. He sees her down by the water, all silhouette, skinny new legs and arms she will grow into. She doesn't know he is watching. She doesn't even know he exists, and that is how it should be.

He goes inside and makes himself a cup of tea. From the window above the sink he can still see her, and she still cannot see him. As it steeps, black with lemongrass, he thinks, as he does every morning, about this ritual. He doesn't even like lemongrass. But she did, and the aroma reminds him of her. The taste is bitter on his tongue.

There's a lovely chill in the air and the porcelain warms his palms. He stirs honey into the cup and watches her from the veranda, stepping in and out of the waves, testing her balance on first one foot and then the other. Only a few more days now, maybe a week.

In the basement, the boy waits. He doesn't know he is a boy yet; he doesn't know anything but his salty chemical bath and the ripple of his hair in the current. Boys take longer than girls, but they come out larger and more fully formed. He won't need the time on the beach that she does. His legs won't need the practice.

His fingertips tingle. Somewhere inside his lizard brain, he remembers the feel of her skin. Elastic, then dough, then paper, then dust. Again and again and again.

Jude I:

Grade school. He drew her comics in art class, and in other classes too. He got in trouble for that, but just a little. It made her smile. It was worth it.

In sixth grade he moved, but in ninth there she was again in his neighborhood, for just a few months, just for summer camp, and then it turned out that her uncle lived a few houses down, so he saw her sometimes.

College: he forgot about her, mostly, in the haze of studying science and art and other girls. Once he was home for Christmas and went to the bar with Thom Waterson and he saw her through a beery visage, sitting with her uncle and two cousins, dressed like a Christmas cracker and probably not as drunk as he. He told Thom Waterson he thought she was beautiful, but Thom died in a car crash that New Year's Eve.

First jobs, a handful of moves, a flicker of girlfriends, but he would see her on the subway, on the street, on television infomercials where he knew she couldn't be. And then one day he opened his door to find her unlocking the apartment across from his, like she was fated to be there, like he had just been waiting all this time to come home.

Jude II:

On the beach, a chance encounter. A girl, pretty but coltish, not yet fully grown. She was familiar. He thought maybe he knew her, slightly, a family friend.

Later he couldn't stop thinking about her. She was all angles; triangle nose, kited elbows, boxy knees. Teeth too large, but still alluring. They glowed in his mind like candy.

The beach, again, but later still, he could not say how much. She looked older, softer, the lines of her body blurred into something wet and mammalian. They spoke, sentences light as eiderdown, void of substance but full of warmth.

And later, sunset, night, sunrise, days and weeks and months and years, the heat of his body twinned with hers, all mouth and hand and skin and hair.

Jude III:

Hello.

Hello.

Do you live nearby?

I do, but-

It's just, you look a little lost.

Do I?

You're just standing there, staring.

My apologies, you just look so familiar-

Do I?

You do.

That's funny.

Is it?

No, I mean, I was just thinking the same thing. Have we met?

Just now.

I'm Isla.

Jude.

Jude.

Yes.

Jude IV:

Are you waiting for me? Jude. Jude? I'm here. You can stop looking.

Jude V:

Something isn't right. Five is just down there, circling her. Not talking. And as for her, she doesn't even seem to see him. There should be stolen glances by now, at least. The Fours were already naked, sliding along each other and into the waves. Probably an anomaly, but still-

Five growls, low in his belly. He doesn't want talk, but he wants her to notice him. He moves nearer, growls again, louder, higher up, lets it move into his throat, warm his chest, explode out through his mouth and nose and eyes. He can feel the sound still buzzing in his ears, after he stops. She notices him now.

He leaves the tea and goes down to the basement to check the levels. Did he measure wrong? His eyes are tired. He needs new glasses. His chest knocks twice, hard.

"Hello?" she says, "Are you okay?" She almost trips. Her legs are shaking, straining, and it excites him. Five grunts low, warm, cold.

She backs away a little, but there is only the sea behind her.

He notes her unfocused eyes, her glassy gaze. Maybe it would be better to wait, give her more time.

He taps the glass. It's too dark down here today. Maybe a storm moving in. Six is still growing like he should be. Maybe a little slower. He's not sure. The calendar doesn't look right. Did he forget to rip a page off yesterday? What about the day before? He tears two, just in case, then a third. Throws the whole thing into the trash. Can it really be September already?

Five can't wait.

"What did you say?" she asks. She looks frightened, but that isn't right, but it's all he has, so he grunts at her again, a whisper, a roar, the only word he can think.

Run.

Six is fine. His vitals are within the normal range. Time to check on Five.

She runs, but she's slow, so he gives her a head start. When she rounds the bend and he can almost no longer see her he gives chase, and catches her, easily.

She's so soft.

He finds her on the beach, but not the usual beach. She's mangled beyond repair, blood washing out with the waves. Five stands nearby, mewling, his mouth and hands red, his belly distended. He falls to his knees in the sand, even knowing he will have trouble getting back up.

He does not usually allow himself to interact with them after they are released, but Five has already seen him. He touches what is left of her skin, and he shudders. He is not allowed to touch her. She is not for him, not this one, but look what has happened.

Five comes closer, but he creeps, he hunches, he doesn't walk like a man. There is something wrong with this one. He will have to check Six's levels again tonight.

He strokes Isla's hair. It is just as he remembered, and he's lost.

Five touches him gently, smears his shirt sleeve with her blood. He takes his hand. She always dies too early, but not like this, never like this.

Five brings his fingers to his lips and for a moment he is afraid that he will be next, but then he understands; that this was not an act of hate, but an act of hunger; of desire to consume what is most loved, and for a moment he is jealous that he never thought of this before it was too late, because now she is a part of Five forever.

He strokes Five's jaw with his thumb. Has it always been this pronounced? There is stubble growing gently there, gravel beneath his skin. He embraces him, briefly, and Five clings for a moment like a child, even helps him stand.

He thinks that maybe he should let this one go. It was so fast this time. But it would be too cruel to let him live without her.

He takes out the gun and notices his hand tremble, even though he cannot feel it.

Five will not know guns, but surely he can sense what is about to happen. But he does not look away, and soon his blood runs out with hers.

He buries them with the others. It takes him all night. When he is done, all he wants to do is fall into bed, but first he must shower, burn the clothes too stained with blood and earth to recompense.

Dawn breaks again, and the leaves are falling now. He greets them with a glass of bourbon, gold to match their gold. His muscles ache. He cleans his glasses, all alone again.

It's early, but he will release the girl. He can feel his internal clock fill to bursting, and he needs to see her one last time.

She is so small. Smaller than even the last one. He will give her extra time before he lets out Six. She watches him warily, but warms at the sight of food, the smell of tea. Lemongrass mingles with the salt air. She breathes in deep, wrinkles her nose. He has a lump in his throat no amount of swallowing can dislodge.

He leaves her to her explorations. Brews himself a cup. Drags his weary body to the verandah again, but he cannot see her. Perhaps she is still sitting there, watching the water like him. The thought makes him smile, gives him enough energy to drag himself upwards once more, then down to the basement to check Six.

Six looks normal. Six looks like Five, and Four, and all the rest. Like a mirror. He makes a few adjustments, sets the timer to remind himself a few days hence.

His chest knocks again, and he feels himself slipping, and then Six is above him, eyes closed, limbs floating. Floating. There is a roar of unbearable pain, but it only makes him laugh.

At last, he thinks, then grimaces, aches, stretches and unfolds and collapses in on himself.

Isla, I'm coming.

Jude VI:

A noise. Loud and muffled. He shakes his head, feels something dislodge. The noise is louder. Piercing. Shrilling. He cannot breathe.

A struggle. He flails his limbs and it feels good to move. Feels right. His lungs hurt. He kicks out as hard as he can and his muscles spring into action.

He slides. There is brief pain but there is also air, and he lays gasping in it. The noise still. When he's had his fill he tries to stand, finds he can, finds whatever is making that scream, and hits it until it stops.

Silence.

In the semi darkness he feels his way around. Is he blind? He climbs over something on the floor, a round lump. Then something sharp; his knees and feet prickle and stab, but he keeps going, hands outstretched.

Smooth, rough, metal, plastic, things he doesn't have words for. He finds stairs and climbs them, fumbles with the door's unfamiliar latch and then it is light, so bright he cannot see at first, but at least it means he isn't blind.

More doors, more stairs, more things with no names, and then, all at once, he is outside, and he can smell it, salty, familiar, he is drawn to it like a magnetic north, and then it's all around him, and it stings, and it fills his nose and eyes and lungs and it's just like earlier when he couldn't breathe only now there's nothing to flail against, his legs and arms are useless, they do not do what he tells them to, but then there is a hand on his arm, two hands, grabbing and pulling and throwing him to the shore.

She looks strong.

"Oh," she says. "You're not him."

All he can do is lay there and cough, staring up at her. The sun rises behind her, making her glow.

She kneels by him, helps him sit.

"Are you all right?" she asks.

When he can breathe again, he nods. Salt streams off his hair in rivers, it feels wonderful.

"You were expecting someone else?" he says. It is the first time he has spoken, and his voice surprises him with its depth, with the purr he feels within his chest as he releases it to the air.

"No," she says, "I don't know. You looked like someone else to me. It doesn't matter."

"I'm Jude," he says, the name dredged up from somewhere inside him. How does he know?

"Isla," she says. She stands, extends a hand to help him up. He grabs her and their palms fit together, so well.

She's leading him down a path, and it takes him a moment to realize it's the same way he came down to the water. He can see his bloody footprints, he follows them back like a map.

"I found this house a few days ago," she tells him. "Until then I just lived on the beach. But it's cold at night. It's much nicer inside." They reach the front door, and it's broken.

"Someone's been here!" she says.

"It was me," he points out his footprints. He must have broken the handle as he fumbled out.

"You're bleeding." She leads him to a chair, puts his feet on her lap. The waves have washed the broken glass clean, but his blood stains her fingers as she probes. It hurts, but he likes that she is touching him. She wraps a towel around each foot.

"Does it hurt?" she asks. He shakes his head.

"When did you get here?" she asks him. "Where did you come from?"

"The basement," he says. He slides on toweled feet back to the door, still open. There is a light switch at the top, and they turn it on together, descend the stairs side by side.

"Careful of the glass," he whispers, although now he sees that she is wearing shoes, and clothes, and he wears nothing but towels. He feels his face heat, but she does not seem to notice.

"There's someone down there," she says, then louder, "Hello? Are you alright?"

There is someone lying on the ground, but he isn't listening. This must be the thing he climbed over, round and soft. They roll him over and Isla gasps, a little sound like a wave.

"It's him," she whispers, but when she looks at Jude her forehead lines.

"It's you," she says. She touches the man's cheek, then Jude's. Her skin is elasticy and warm and he wants to push his whole face into her hand but she pulls away. "He looks just like you."

They go upstairs and she shows him a mirror, and she's right, he looks like the man in the basement, but somehow younger, newer.

"Is it your father?" she asks, but he doesn't know.

They find a place to bury him, a nice flat field not too far from the house. There are other graves there, set up in pairs, their headstones nothing but numbers. There is a space next to number one, so they decide that must be where he belongs.

Digging is hard work, but they are both young and strong. Some of his cuts open up again while they work.

When they go inside she shows him how she has learned to turn on the shower, and to his surprise she joins him under the water, her body so different but yet the same. She helps him wash the scratches on his back, and when they get out they find gauze beneath the sink, and she wraps it around his wounds.

In the bedroom there are clothes which fit him loose around the waist. She has her own in a box on the floor. They lay next to each other on the bed and wonder together.

When he awakens he finds she has made tea, something bitter that he does not care for but drinks down because she has made it. On the table beside the bed is a photo, and the people in the frame look like him and Isla, though he knows they can't be.

They clean up the basement together. It is much better with shoes. They wonder at the use of the machines and tubes and vials of liquids. There is whole fridge with small containers labeled with stick figures. Half have a triangle body, half a square.

He finds he wants to touch her, but she always moves away before he has a chance.

They are learning to cook. He has figured out how to light the stove. They make many experiments, some are good and some are not. They try everything, even the brown bottle that makes them dizzy.

The island is not very big, and they know every inch of it. They learn what they can eat and what they can't. They catch animals, and sometimes fish, rarely birds. The small ones they catch they let go, and catch again later when they are grown.

Hidden in a drawer is a book of photos, of the other Isla and Jude. In the beginning they look like the real Isla and Jude, but by the end of the book Isla is withered and sickly.

"Is this the future?" Isla wonders, "Is this what will happen to me?" He hopes not. He does not want to lose her.

One night he finds her in the kitchen, weeping. Her throat hurts, she says, her face is hot. He touches her *at last!* and she is burning. She is frightened, he is terrified. He carries her outside, where it is cool, where snow is falling. He wraps his arms around her. He cannot let her go. She is still hot, and he helps her remove her clothes, and he removes his as well and they stand together staring towards the beach until he begins to shiver and she wraps her hot body around his and they are no longer standing, but something else, something amazing out here in the snow.

He buries her with the others, but apart. He does not want to give her just a number, so he scratches *Isla* into the stone as best he can. The sun is setting.

He wishes he had more time.

He wishes he had more than a photograph of a woman who looks like her, but is not her.

He wishes he could start over, make another Isla, another Jude, and try again.

Maybe he can.

Hannah Lackoff has been nominated for the Pushcart Prize, and the storySouth Million Writers Award. She has been published in *Spark, Drabblecast, Bourbon Penn, 10,000 Tons of Black Ink* and others. Her short story collection *After the World Ended* was published by 18th Wall Productions. She lives in Boulder, Colorado. Visit her at hannahlackoff.wix.com/writing.

SPACE& SCOTLAND

The new FREE quarterly magazine covering all aspects of space technology and exploration as they relate to Scotland.

PLUS: interviews, guest writers, astronomy, science fiction literature and music.

EDITED BY DUNCAN LUNAN

e: spaceandscotland@actascio.org

ISSUE 1 OUT NOW!

AVAILABLE IN PRINTED AND DIGITAL FORMATS

Goodnight New York, New York

Victoria Zelvin

Despite the numerous public reports otherwise, when Soo-Jung paddled up to where the Chrysler Building was supposed to be, she found it already claimed by the ocean. After circling the shadowed expanse of water twice, she slapped her goggles on, leaned out of her kayak, stuck her face into the water and… yep.

"Well," Soo-Jung said to the lapping waves, salt water streaming down her cheeks.

Caroline's despair translated easily across the garbled radio. It was the only thing that did. "No, n…fifty met…last year!"

Soo-Jung cupped some salt water in her hand and slapped it onto her neck. Official statement from the Office of Monitoring Sea Levels had reported, and been reporting for years, that the Chrysler building remained at least fifty meters above the water in all tides. While the sea had been halted in its gradual approach by the OMSL's levy project, keeping shorelines fairly stagnant, no one truly knew how bad the damage was off shore, on what used to be land. Out of sight, out of mind, that was OMSL's approach to the public. Lock away the former sites, shove them under a giant tarp labeled UNSAFE, and hope the people forget there was ever a place called New York City. It seemed to be working. No one had gotten a non-government sanctioned photo out of New York in at least twenty years and, slowly, those had lessened in frequency as well to nothing for the past two.

"Sea levels must have risen again," she said, but she wasn't sure how much made it through. VHFs were the grandfathers of antiquated maritime technology and theirs, despite numerous repairs and being fused together with equal parts old metal and plastic printed parts, barely cooperated. Even a scant twenty miles away across nothing but ocean, they were scrambled. But everyone, Soo-Jung included, was more worried about OMSL's interference in the name of "safety" and arrests before they're done than reliable communication and so without knowing what was intelligible, Soo-Jung continued into her walkie, "Plus your hurricane swept through. Cat-3 Caroline must've snapped the spire off. Storm surge'd easily swallow fifty meters of building."

"G…mmit."

Twirling her paddle up and down the top of her kayak, Soo-Jung's eyes moved across the shadowed expanse of ocean to an above water spire. Soo-Jung held down the transmit button. "There's not much of it left, but the Empire State is still kind of above water," she said. "Think Empire State'll work just as well. Slanted, but I think I can get in and tuck the kayak inside," she concluded. The original plan had been to shelter within the walls of the Chrysler building, to tuck the kayak inside so it wouldn't be snapped by satellites while she was under, and dive. The street-by-street plan would suffer from the difference, but in theory New York was easy to navigate.

There was a long pause from the other end, then: "…e care…"

Half sure that meant *be careful*, Soo-Jung responded, "Sure. Out."

With a small sigh to clear her lungs, Soo-Jung dipped her paddle back into the water and twisted her kayak to face the dilapidated Empire State building. A good amount of the famous building remained above water, the familiar arches currently covered in gulls and their nests, and bent decidedly backwards.

Soo-Jung had to break a window to get inside. Seagulls shrieked at her as she slid the kayak inside, finding more nestlings burrowed into the decayed drywall. "Nice birdies," she urged, though she knew they were not. She wound a length of rope around the bow of her kayak and tied it to an exposed metal girder just below the surface, stepping onto it to prepare. Even though her specialized skin weave would allow her to withstand the pressure and protect her internal organs, it was still going to be damned cold down there. The wetsuit was tight, uncomfortable, and hard to zip up alone, but she managed with only a few derogatory remarks to the yapping gulls, then pulled on gloves and little swim socks. She would swim faster frog kicking than she ever would with flippers.

Hand in hand with the weave that had thickened her skin was the procedure to reconstruct and strengthen her inner ear. For this project she'd tested the depth at five hundred meters, diving with other specifically-enhanced divers off the coast of Maui. While there, she'd also tested the most experimental and crucial aspect to her dive here: the alteration of her myoglobin in her muscle tissue. Specially infused with whale DNA, she'd sucked in a single breath before diving in Maui and lasted a full hour under the water.

She and Caroline had gone back and forth on this for months. The camera was a required, absolutely vital part of the mission. Anything else risked tripping the scanners. Hence, the kayak taken paddled out from the larger boat safe in international waters. Hence, the VHF's. No diving apparatus still existed without a network connection and a host of electronics set to ensure as few drowning deaths as could be possible. They'd talked about 3D printing some, just a basic tank and some rubber, but in the end it had been easier to simply genetically engineer Soo-Jung into the ability to hold her breath underwater for the duration of the dive.

It was… troubling, though. She sat herself down on the girder a moment, forcing herself to breathe in the exercises the doctors had taught her, to count as the freedivers had advised, until her heartrate was marginally under control. If this was to work, she'd need her heart to beat slowly, not the other way around. Soo-Jung took her time, trying to find her calm even if she had to repeat the words *find calm* silently over and over. When she half-way believed it, she lashed her camera to her belt.

So far, so good, so haven't been arrested yet.

Soo-Jung stood up on the girder, her legs unsteady underneath her. "Dear God," she said, voice reverberating in the hollow cavern. "I would really appreciate it if I didn't drown. Amen."

She walked on the girder out to the window and hopped out the window, sinking below the waves.

The first thing she did was to take several barely sub-subsurface pictures of the view from the Empire State, over the ghastly shadows the buildings made in the water, testing her breath hold. She surfaced several times, sucking in deeper breaths, and sinking down further each time, ghosting alongside the dilapidated buildings. They scarce looked real, ruins just meters under the water. They grew more concrete to her gaze as she swam down, pausing every few floors to peer out at the city and to snap a photo, trying to work her nerve up.

She made one last trip to the surface, sucking in three quick gulps of air, before diving for real, straight down the side of the Empire State, following the lines the sun cut through the water until they faded almost entirely.

The main project was an artistic one, to dive down and take pictures of the sites of famous photos. The camera was preprogrammed with images and Soo-Jung was to take one picture as it was, then to line up the underwater of now with the scenery of the past to show the change. As she dove, her heart began to pound out a rhythm against her ribs. This hardly felt illegal, and yet…

Soo-Jung mentally crossed the Chrysler Building off her list, instead swimming away from the Empire State towards a spot she'd had picked out for herself.

It took some time to find the New York Public Library, what remained of it, and when she did Soo-Jung fumbled for her camera, fingers numb already. Some of the columns had fallen, a school of silver fish descending through them to go inside, but the sign remained at the base of the stairs. Soo-Jung pulled the photo of her great-grandmother up on her camera, and held the viewer up to her eye so she could laboriously line up her shot, trying to find the column that her great-grandmother had been leaning up against.

Her great-grandmother had made her way to New York on her own. While she never managed to scrape up enough money to go to school, like she wanted, her great-grandmother spent most of her life in the library. She was one of the last to leave the city, and had campaigned to evacuate the books as the city began to flood. In the photo she was young, sixteen, blushing as the wind blew her hair into her face. Soo-Jung wanted to swim further, inside the library perhaps, but salt water had begun to gather in her eyes and she could not afford to let it leak into her goggles. Her chest felt tight enough that she blew out a small bubble of air, just to calm herself. She swam away without daring to look back.

She had photos to take that she and Caroline had actually planned to take.

Times Square was the priority, and Soo-Jung had picked three inserts to shoot. The first was the V-J Day kiss. The second showed the crowds assembled to watch the first human step onto the surface of Mars. The third photo was the last New Year's Eve in New York, an illegal party thrown in freezing waist deep water to watch the ball drop one last time. Soo-Jung found that same ball shattered on the ocean floor and discovered upon investigation that a family of crabs that had moved inside. She shone her flashlight upon them and disturbed them the few moments it took to take a photo. A large crab raised his claws at her as she backed away, snapping in the water, and she snorted to think he might have been saying, *we own these streets.*

She moved on. Madison Square Garden was hard to find, and harder to photograph, so little was left. A shark approached her shot of Radio City Music Hall, and Soo-Jung snapped a few pictures as he drew near. He passed her by close enough that she could reach out and pet his rough skin, to which he flicked his tail in her face and swam lazily off. The light of the camera's review screen was bright enough to hurt her eyes, but she smiled see this shark swim around her insert photo of some Rockettes on a smoke break.

From the Music Hall, Soo-Jung swam over what remained of 30 Rock towards the Cathedral, the camera bouncing against her side with every wide arching frog kick. She was getting cold even through her wetsuit, and she tried to keep shaking her limbs out under the water to compensate. Saint Patrick's was in good enough shape that she could snap several photos of her insert, struck by the spires cutting through the dim sunbeams underwater. Grand Central Station was in slightly better shape than Madison Square Garden, but she doubted the photo of would live up to Caroline's standards. The insert Caroline had picked was of scores of refugees waiting for the evacuation buses, and the columns they filed between were now little more than sand.

From Grand Central, she swam her way leisurely down Lexington Avenue, soaking in the ambiance of the city. She only made her way up toward the surface once she could touch the Empire State building, using it as a measure of how fast she rose, careful to go slow.

Breaking the surface was exhilarating, a flash of warmth upon her face, and the sudden influx of new oxygen made her dizzy. Her heart rate came back up rapidly, pulsing out a seeming protest for her exertions right up against her temple. She flipped onto her back, lazily kicking her legs until she reentered the Empire State building back floating. She still spent a good hour inside the Empire State laying in the small pool made by the girder, legs hanging on either side, letting her heart rate come down.

"Be back soon," she lied into her walkie, pushing her long kayak back to a time when she could sit up without being dizzy.

*

The sun was nearly under the horizon by the time Soo-Jung paddled up alongside the boat Caroline had rented for the day's "fishing" trip. Half anticipating the Coast Guard to materialize, Soo-Jung grasped Sunil's proffered hand, letting him pull her up onto the deck. Sunil then pulled up the kayak, flexing synthetic muscles and the strength in heavy metal infused bones. Soo-Jung found Caroline under the shaded cabin, bent almost double over her own forearm.

"Anything good?" Soo-Jung asked, humor stolen by her uneven breathing. She had pushed her enhancements hard today. She made a small sweeping gesture at the fishing rods assembled against the railings by the cooler.

"Hm," Caroline spoke up, staring at the screen affixed into her forearm. Soo-Jung knew that Caroline would have eagerly downloaded the photos the moment Soo-Jung was in range. Later tonight, after Caroline had edited them for clarity, they'd be up on the internet.

Soo-Jung grabbed the railing and used it to help her on her way down, grunting and grimacing as she sat. She fell the rest of the way, muscles protesting, pressing her back against the railing. She was going to be sore tomorrow. Also, very possibly arrested. She half wanted to joke about using her prison time to sleep, but a nervous lump had taken up residence in her throat. It was hard to see Caroline's expression through the curtain of her hair.

"I don't think there'll be a single building above the waterline soon," Soo-Jung told Caroline. Her expression was somber, but lightened for a moment to hear the word 'nice' somewhere to her left and treated Sunil with a brief flicker of a smile as she tapped his fist with hers. "It's worse than they're saying," she said, serious once more.

Caroline didn't answer. Sunil made noise about getting them out of there, and Caroline didn't so much as flinch as the boat began to move again, kicking up seawater. Soo-Jung was almost asleep when Caroline finally looked up.

"This is beautiful," Caroline said, swiping her finger up on her screen, turning in her swivel chair to face the large projection. Caroline had brightened it in the few minutes she'd had it, and the picture of Soo-Jung's great-grandmother gleamed in front of the murky library.

"My great-grandmother," Soo-Jung identified, a bit nervously.

Caroline settled back in her chair, crossing her arms over her chest. "We're leading with this one," she said. "Times Square'll be all over everywhere once it's out there," Caroline continued, flipping her hand. "I'll publish it tomorrow. I want this one first. I want it to be personal. Why else did we do this, if it wasn't personal?" She shook her head. "Never really cared about the buildings."

Soo-Jung wiped her eyes on the back of her hand. It made them sting with salt. Sniffing, Soo-Jung smiled. "Me neither."

Victoria Zelvin is a graduate of the inaugural class of Roanoke College's Creative Writing program. Her fiction has previously appeared in publications from Meerkat Press, A Murder of Storytellers, and others. She currently lives just outside Washington DC in Ballston, VA with her one eyed cat, Leela.

The Descendant

Katy Lennon

ENTRY 1

Health and mental stress levels are normal this morning, with the exception of a slight toxin increase. Nothing so extreme so as to cause TOTAL BRAIN SHUTDOWN or even DANGEROUSLY HIGH LEVELS OF CORTISOL, both of which require my emergency intervention protocol to automatically

enable itself.

The problem isn't

that he didn't know what happened, it was that he did fuck

all about it!

I'm telling
you

he needs to know that he's allowed to

help!

John always enjoyed his cup of tea in the morning, with honey instead of sugar. Sugar is much too sweet; honey is just right. I asked John if he would like a cup of tea, to which he replied that he could murder one. (This implies yes.) There was no milk in the fridge, and the milk delivery had not arrived; close examination of the empty milk bottle still standing on the doorstep confirmed this. I told John there was no milk and afterwards I made him some toast. He did not eat it. We had a surplus of bread, so this was an acceptable course of action. We watched the news together, and John told me to pay attention when the news anchor spoke about a government plan to help citizens leave the city. That was the first time this command had been issued to me, so I was unsure of what course of action to take. I have recorded the transcript here:

"…initiative undertaken by First Minister Taylor Singh on Wednesday morning, when she announced to the Scottish Parliament that even though the city remained, quote 'a fortress of familial security and strength' that plans to evacuate the areas closest to the wall's perimeter were 'a purely formal procedure' set out in Edinburgh City Council's Catastrophe Strategy of 2045. Singh compared the evacuation to 'flossing one's teeth in order to prevent tooth decay; a pre-emptive measure'. The FM also urged the public to stay calm and collected in the face of this minor adjustment. Shuttles carrying nearly 5,000 residents of Lower Edinburgh will be leaving the city over the course of the coming weeks, journeying through the Vastus to a government controlled safety zone."

John didn't seem happy about this news, despite designating it as valuable information. This was confusing. I hadn't asked him if he wanted a cup of tea in approximately 2 hours, so I enquired again, and John said he would murder *me* if I asked again. (I didn't ask him again.) I suggested a walk in the garden, or a visit to the vapour therapy room to reduce stress levels, as threats of homicide usually indicate high levels of anger. When John was unresponsive to my suggestions, I asked if he would like to video-call the neighbours; they have a holo-pet programme that he has consistently enjoyed, which is proven to reduce stress levels. But John informed me that the couple had vacated their property, and taken their *bloody* holo-pet with them. I wasn't sure how to respond to this, as

I was sure I had seen

Mr. Finnegan HUMAN FACE DATABASED FOR RECOGNITION, CATEGORIZATION: SAFE

in the garden the previous 28/01/2050 22:57

evening. DATABASE CATEGORIZATION ERROR.

ENTRY 2

I booted up before John woke up, and assessed his health data. I was alerted to the fact that John's heart was under an unprecedented level of strain and, if untreated, could lead to IRREPERABLE HARM. I was glad to have caught this sign early, and was in the process of informing John of his renewed dietary plan when he interrupted me. He told me to get ready to leave. He forced many of his possessions into a bag. I was not sure why he was doing this. I asked, and he told me we were leaving. His tone and body language suggested that he was not in a stable state of mind, and I did not want to aggravate the situation further, so I decided to halt my line of enquiry. We took a taxi to the city limits where there was much commotion; an abnormal number of humans seemed to be trying to leave the city. Since the scheduled evacuation was not due to happen for another few weeks, I found this conflictive with my previously logged information. I reported this to John immediately. John seemed exasperated, and told me that was ages ago, you silly bot, she's done us up proper - now put this on. I put on the scarf even though it limited my ocular capabilities.

We travelled on foot after this point, and I removed the scarf from my eyes to allow safe movement amongst the many humans pressing together. Shortly after this a man put his hand on my shoulder and said alright son, what model are you then? You should have been scrap metal years ago. But I'm sure there's still something in you we can use.

I wasn't sure what the man meant but it upset John, as he grabbed me with higher levels of force than necessary and said to the man get your hands off my son

you see officer

we really see him as a son, we don't have the heart

to just get rid of him look he meant

no harm by it really, we'll have him

repaired and he'll

be back up to scratch in no time.

I was not the man's son, so I was unclear on why he had referred to me as such. I asked John about it but he did not reply, he only led us deeper into the crowd. I told John that I remembered

Wilma had been wearing a yellow dress the day the police came.

ENTRY 3

We boarded a bus, even though a lot of people were displaying signs of anger and contempt towards us for doing so. We sat at the back, and John insisted I wear the scarf over my face. We drove approximately 370//90//3 miles past the wall and into the Vastus. I knew we were beyond the wall because my data signal dropped by 79%. I read high levels of epinephrine on the bus, and many passengers were experiencing DANGEROUSLY HIGH LEVELS OF CORTISOL in their nervous systems. I began to formulate and present a plan of action to help combat this. The person sitting next to me had the highest levels of epinephrine, and a large rage spike caused him to remove the scarf from my head, and shout. He's a bloody bot! Kids were shoved out of the way to get this wanker on the bus and he's got a fucking Plaisim with him! This caused a large disturbance. Many people were shouting that we shouldn't be allowed on the bus. The same man who had taken the scarf off of my head implied that I was only there to supply John with sexual stimulation. (Specifically oral stimulation.) One woman said that I should be left behind with them. The other passengers agreed with her.

John did not agree with the woman. He stood up and said he didn't know what they were talking about, this is my son, he's been looking after me. He has just as much right as anyone else to be on this bus he has the right to live, doesn't he?

He's not a real person, John.

that doesn't mean you get to just buy a new son

I told John I remembered ERROR DATABASE CORRUPTION. The passengers were becoming increasingly more anxious, and I assessed that the risk of violent behaviour had risen by 106%. Upon further assessment I concluded that my absence from the bus would reduce the risk of a potentially unmanageable situation. COMPLETE DATA CORRUPTION. I am a Plaisim 0200. My operating system is recommended for young families. I have a running time of twelve hours per day when properly charged and regularly debugged. I can assist in such tasks as cooking and cleaning, as well as the mental and physical care of humans aged 0 months and up. My recommended retail price is. My life expectancy is. My memory capabilities typically last. My operating system is recommended for young families.

ENTRY 4

I had logged knowledge of the land outside the wall, as it was frequently discussed on John's preferred news channel. LEVELS OF DISCARDED TECH REACHING DANGEROUS LEVELS IN THE VASTUS, A SAD REMINDER OF OUR SOCIETY'S DISPOSABLE CULTURE. ECOLOGISTS SAY WE HAVE "RUINED" OUR CHANCES OF RETURNING TO THE OUTSIDE WORLD. RUMOURS OF "VASTUS SQUATTERS" FUEL TO FIRE AMID VIRUS OUTBREAKS.

John's mental, and physical, state was not improving. This meant he had reduced capabilities for effective stamina. My primary directive enforcers were approaching emergency overdrive mode. In this setting I am forced to apply the appropriate medical treatment to my primary user, consent not required. John did not give me his consent. Despite his hazardously low energy levels he persisted in navigating the complex paths in between dangerous sharp metals and chemicals, some of which included: steel, aluminium casing, polycarbonate plastics, unrea-formaldehyde, volatile organic compounds, the wool jumper that John kept under his pillow, it smells like he smelled can you bloody believe it

Journey destination unclear.

Commands unclear.

What is my primary function? I asked John, and he told me to just keep moving, we couldn't stay here for too long [COUGH – INDICATES RESPIRATORY PROBLEMS//SEEK MEDICAL ATTENTION] I did not understand why. I told him I had recognized several human-designated life forms concealed within the structures surrounding us. John told me that was the problem. DATA CORRUPTION UNPROCESSED COMMAND. HUMAN LIFE FORMS DATABASED, DESIGNATION: SAFE. UNABLE TO RECATEGORIZE: CONFLICTING INFORMATION, PRIMARY DIRECTIVE COMPROMISED.

I asked John when we were going to go home. I asked John if he would like a cup of tea. John said we weren't going home. I asked John if he would like a cup of tea. My processors analysed our surroundings, and concluded that there were no human-suitable spaces within a 3.5 mile radius. 0 properties in the surrounding area contained holographic capabilities, nourishment rehydration stations or suitable capacities for rest or sleep. This did not seem to trouble John. He said desperate times call for desperate measures. (I wasn't sure how to reply.)

"Extremis malis extrema remedia" – Erasmus

"For extreme diseases, extreme methods of cure, as to restriction, are most suitable." – Hippocrates

John did not reply.

John crawled inside and abandoned PodHotel 50 sleeper pod structure, manufactured 2029, company fell into disuse 2033. 89% of its surface area was covered in rust. I advised John against entering, as it could provoke several dangerous outcomes. Stability was not assured. John ordered me to enter the pod next to him, to lie down, shut up and go to sleep. I obeyed, and activated sleep mode. My primary directive enforcers reminded me that although sleep mode saves energy, it reduces my sensory capabilities by over 80%.

ENTRY 5

I booted up at my assigned hour. John was not in the pod next to me. When I exited the pod John was pacing back and forth; his anger levels had reached intolerable intensities. I could read his health stats but they did not make any sense. They resembled the ones I had read in the structures the previous day. I approached him in order to apply my anti-stress chemical compound; my primary directive enforcers had taken hold. Upon further inspection I observed that John's clothing and skin was covered in blood. Tactile samples were taken, and the results concluded that only some of it was his own. I asked John what had happened. He did not respond. There was a large quantity of blood on the ground around him, as well as some indecipherable human remains. They had not been there the day before.

John looked at me but did not display facial recognition traits. I enacted my second attempt at performing my primary directive. John used uncategorized sounds to express how he felt about this. TRANSLATION: Black bear alert call, fox alarm bark, wolf warning growl, vixen's scream. I did not understand why John's vocal capabilities had become compromised. His aggression levels were high enough to classify the situation as DANGEROUSLY VOLATILE. I continued to implement my primary directive. John bit me on the arm. No grievous harm induced. I continued to implement my primary directive. Human remains slid from John's mouth. I continued to implement my primary directive. I recognized the remains as one of the women from the bus. The wedding ring. My primary directive is to provide both mental and physical care to my primary user as well as other humans. My primary directiveMy primary directive. My primary directive is to help John. *Help, John! Help me!*

She didn't die in the hospital. She died on the living room floor. I read her heart rate as it slowed down and stopped.

He just needs to know better, for next time. You never know what might happen.

It's that thing's bloody fault, not mine! He was supposed to help us, not just stand there while…

Guess it's just you and me now, son.

Son.

END TRANSCRIPT

Although this particular document obviously contains many continuity issues as well as factual errors, it proved pivotal in myself and my colleagues' study of the events of the summer of 2050. This AI's lifetime log was exemplary of the kind of primary text we were looking for – Chief Document Recovery Agent Dr Samara Wright.

THIS DOCUMENT IS FOR OFFICIAL WORLD HEALTH ORGANIZATION USE ONLY AND MUST REMAIN PRIVATE AND CONFIDENTIAL. NOT FOR INTERPLANETARY USE.

Katy Lennon is a new sci-fi and horror writer originally from Aberdeen, now based in Edinburgh. She writes about the future, posthumanism and artificial intelligence. She also maintains the illusion that her constant social media presence is purely for research purposes. Follow Katy on Twitter @blooood_bath

---

Wallace
West

The Worm

Russell Jones

Art: Wallace West

The kids drop today's worm onto their tongues, the bell rings, and they swallow.

"Is that it for today?"

You'd think, after all these sessions, they'd have learned something for themselves. Tests always come after the worm on Mondays. "No, we've a quiz. Now take out your pads."

They let out a collective hum, like wasps in a jar.

I push the button and the test begins; Doctor Hello appears at the front of the class, his blue skin and lab coat shimmering. My finger throbs, I rub it and imagine a bolt passing through Doctor Hello's blue brains, my gun purring, a grin across my face.

"Hello class!" Doctor Hello says, cheerily.

"Hello Doctor!"

"Today's quiz will begin shortly. If you haven't taken your worm, please take it now." Doctor Hello turns to me. "Your teacher will confirm when you are ready."

"Confirm." I slide my finger across my screen, pretending to work. I think the kids are onto me, they've caught me more than once – my movements are too frantic for work, my eyes are too keen. I look up from the screen; the kids are busy absorbing the worm that sits in their stomachs, melting like ice in a glass of bourbon. I still get a buzz from seeing the knowledge slither forward, the spark in each of them as their brains feed. It's something most teachers take pleasure in: progress.

Everyone remembers their first worm, and their most recent. My first worm was later than most – I was six, just out of Socialisation Class. Toy bricks, circuits, the usual. I held that little blue pill in my hand, tears ploughing down my cheeks.

"Don't worry," my mum said. "We all do it."

When you're six, that's not a reassurance. I knew my world, I liked my ignorance. I refused.

"There are ways around it, don't be concerned." The Socialisation leader told my mum. I should have been more suspicious when a bowl of ice cream, scattered with blue sweeties, arrived as a treat after dinner that night.

The worm creeps up on you. At first you don't notice it, you just trail off into a stream of thoughts you didn't know existed. Then BANG, your head feels different, clearer, like you've lived someone else's life, the years compressed into seconds. You're aware of things you hadn't noticed before, you see things a bit differently, understand them. That's the only way I can describe it; our poets have done no better.

"Quiz question six." Doctor Hello interrupts my daydream. "In the helio state, which molecule is persistent with the following data..." His question is muted by my incomprehension. I've not taken today's worm yet. I should – we're easily caught out by the smarter kids. I push a button and the printer dispenses a cup of cream. I place the worm in my palm, still holding the apprehensions of my youth, and knock it back.

The kids are busy swiping their answers. I see them growing more confident as the worm takes hold. They probably know more than me now, having had the worm their whole life, but they're still kids. Just. Our records say that some of them, the brightest and best, the High Ups, even took worm pre-birth. No doubt that altered the heliocropic enzymes in their blood, any iron deficits bonding with the chemodata. Ah, I'm starting to absorb today's worm, too.

The test is over. I send Doctor Hello back to his dark dimension in the network, a stone of power rolling in my stomach as I extinguish him. The results flash up on the desks, each kid listed by their performance and average. There are woops, high fives, a few sniffles, a few sniggers. The usual names are at the top, the usual ones at the bottom. No surprises.

"Is that it for today, Doctor?" A kid asks.

I check the time and today's air toxicity. Fine. "Yes, off you go."

"Bye!"

They swarm out of the classroom and into the halls. I chant ancient dialogue from a drama I absorbed through another worm, trying to block out the impending rush of chemodata:

"The man who makes an appearance in the business world, the man who creates personal interest, is the man who gets ahead. Be liked and you will never want. You take me, for instance. I never have to wait in line to see a buyer. Willy Loman is here! That's all they have to know and I go right through..."

"Be liked and you will never want. Act 1, Part 3." Doctor Sabre leans my door, smirking.

"Yep. At least, I think so." I rub my finger. "Waiting for the worm to pass."

"Sorry, want me to go?"

"No, it's fine." I squeeze my eyes shut as the data eases off. Modular compounds, axis draughts, temporal variants. I'm done with the lot. I open my eyes and smile. "What a bore."

"Today's almost put me to sleep." Doctor Sabre motions towards the door and I follow, obediently. "Still, it has its uses." We head towards the staffroom, windows pointing the way. "This new curriculum is a killer."

"Headaches?"

"Not for me, some of my kids though. Two had to go without worms last week. I think their parents were pushing them too hard, they got frazzled. Poor bastards."

"It's a race; they don't want to be left behind."

The human stench of the staff room hits us; a gorilla cage of stale sweat and acid breath. We print our caffeine and then recede to our usual dark corner. Some of the Physicals are stretching, some are competing to see who can outmanoeuvre the other's yoga stance. Doctor Abs is performing a one-handed handstand, her legs parted, feet rotating slowly, humming like a moron. Most of the Academics hover around the printer, filling themselves with sugars and caffeines, talking through the day's worm. The Head, a pompous, irritatingly articulate mound of muscle, is schmoozing. She doesn't like me.

"Okay, okay!" The Head whistles like we're a pack of dogs. "Over here! Settle down. Thank you."

I turn to Sabre and whisper, "Woof." She smiles and pretends to pant, her tongue lolling, before turning her attention to The Head.

"I've reviewed the recent results. Most are on target, but some are slipping. The High Ups aren't doing as well as we'd anticipated. Please, people, make sure you're sticking to the three D's: Data, Diet and..." The Head dangles the word like a fishing hook.

We all bite. "Diagnosis."

"Watch out, we have a duty of care here, people. Now, here's the latest from MediGov. Arms and legs inside the ride!" The Head laughs at her own lame joke, again. She pushes a button and Doctor Hello's bald, glinting blue head appears at the centre of the room.

"Dear Staff, MediGov have vital new information..."

I drown him out in a slurp of caffeine. Doctor Hello always has information to share, none of it vital. I look at Sabre, who catches my glance, smiles and nudges my arm, before her attentions return to Doctor Hello's updates. The Physicals are in ridiculous poses, balancing almost-impossibly on limbs and digits. Today's worm has finished absorbing, but my gut twists and stings like I've been shot in the stomach. I breathe slowly, sucking in a lung of sweaty air, and feel the bile rise in my throat. Gotta get out. I stand.

"You okay?" Sabre asks.

I whisper, not wanting to attract attention. "Yeh, just need air. Worm's down the wrong hole."

She smiles and I bolt to the door, heaving my breakfast onto the corridor floor. The kids will get a kick out of that, at least. I stare at the half-digested mounds of cereals and fruit, frothing in my acids, until the Janitor arrives and instructs me to "Please vacate. Biohazard."

The Janitor sucks my breakfast into him and trundles into a recharge port, I wipe my mouth just in time for the kids to return. This afternoon I have 2B, my least favourite group.

I have a free period before lunch, so walk to the computer labs, sit and pretend to work. Ads flash up for vacations I can't afford, clothes I hate the look of, content I dare not look at on school premises, discounts on worms.

LEARN ALL THE NEW WORLD LANGUAGES! 2 WORMS, 2 HOURS.

BECOME ONE WITH THE ANCIENT WORLD! THE COMPLETE WORKS OF SHAKESPEARE, WITH NOTES, IN JUST 1 WORM.

MILITARY STRATEGY. 1 WORM. BE THE BEST!

BOOKWORM! THE SKILLS SALE! HALF PRICE WORMS FOR ALL OUR SKILLS BOOKS! NOW INCLUDES MARTIAL ARTS FROM GRANDMASTERS, POETRY FROM THE POLARS, AND DATING FOR DUMMIES!

My finger twitches over the offers, but I close them and load my books. It's considered avant garde to read at the moment, something that only artists and time wasters would bother with, but I still bother. I read before it was cool – that's what I tell the kids. They think it's pointless, and I agree sometimes. It would have taken years to learn the medical set, but the course of five worms (and a top up practical session) gave me enough knowledge to take this job. I can fix most things around the house if I need to, we all can. I even learned how to gamble, but didn't have the knack for it. But taking a worm isn't the same as reading a book for yourself – something happens, I get involved. It's like walking around someone's house, checking out their photos, trying on their clothes, drinking their juice. The worm takes all of that away; it feels like you have the blueprints in your hands but never went inside for yourself. I miss the experience.

I swipe the screen and the page turns.

"Hey granddad." Sabre's hands rub my shoulders. I jerk, as if caught watching dodgy ads, and swipe the book away.

"Hey," I turn around, breaking her grip.

"You okay now? Saw the Janitor emptying the contents of your stomach into the flashbins."

"I'm fine, thanks. That Janitor's a blabbermouth."

"I'm just sneaky, that's all. So, you heard the news?"

"No, what?"

"New worms for the High Ups, and settlers to help with any side effects."

Waves of nausea rise and sink in me again. "How can we afford that?" There were cuts, always cuts, and worms were expensive. Giving the brighter kids extra worms and settlers would cost a fortune.

"Parents have to pay. Fifty-fifty expenses split with MediGov."

"Don't fancy the chances of the Low Downs, then."

"Me neither. Should we say something?"

Doctor Hello's cobalt head turns on the windows. He blinks at us. "Nah. They'll trial it, decide it's expensive and stop it. They always do."

"True." She shuffles. "Right, I've a task for you."

"Joy."

"You've got to take these to Sanctum School. The air's fine, so I'd go now."

"Says who?"

"Her headiness. The Head."

Damned Head. "What about class? I've got 2B this afternoon."

Sabre sighs. "I'll take them. We've got to follow orders." She salutes jokingly. "Just pray that I make it out of 2B alive."

"You'll be fine." I grin, happy to be rid of them.

Sanctum School's across the city, but the weather's fine. I stroll, eager to take in as much sunlight as I can before the clouds return. Janitors suck up streaks of dust from the paths, wiping windows so that the ads are clear. The briefcase is lighter than it looks; reinforced alloy, photon strapped to my wrist, packed with excess worms, a tiny ocean of them locked away. It would be less conspicuous without the strap but thefts are up lately, and the newscasters are eager to tell us about the dreaded reality of the world. "Stay In. Don't Take Risks. Watch Out For Deadheads." All the usual jargon we only half believe, and it's dissolved by a walk in the open air.

Sanctum's not too far but I don't fancy the Low Down side of town – too many Deadheads, too unpredictable. I run through the city maps I've memorised, checking the route. Heaven Park will take longer but it's scenic; I'll take it.

The park's brass gate welcomes me, its golden arches stretching high, gentle music willowing through the blades of grass and tree branches. A window reminds me to "Stick to the path (on pain of electrocution)" and I do. There are no Janitors, the floor and plants are already dusted clean, the stimulant birds tweet in their nests – *Four Seasons* by Vivaldi, I think, but I've not taken the Classical Music worm. They flutter their luminescent wings, scales glimmering like the real birds from the days before the clouds. I stand, close my eyes, lose myself in their song for a moment, before I fall to the floor.

"Get it! GET IT!"

"Shit, hurry!"

"Got it!"

The alarm is all I remember fully, and their faces. Two of them: one male, huge, muscular, deep black eyes, a sharp chin. The other: female, ruby red haired, green aug eyes. I tell the police everything I recall. They seem surprised.

"Not the usual suspects." The officer tells me, standing beside my hospital bed. "Unusual. What did they take?"

"Worms."

"Any particular kind?"

"I don't think so. Just educational ones, high school."

"Thank you, you've been a great help. We'll find them. Sorry about your hand."

"Thanks."

Sabre enters as the cops leave, a look of sympathy on her face, holding a data card for the printer.

"Chocolates and grapes, I hope you like them." She inserts the data card and prints a small plate of dessert. "I'm not peeling them for you." She throws a grape into her mouth and chews, then forces a chocolate between my lips.

"Thanks."

"So, how's the hand? Did you get a good look at them?"

I pull the sheet from my mound of flesh, where my hand is being rebuilt. "Fine, it takes a week they said. Recycled nanites, but I'll be back to normal."

"A week off, nice. All doped up?"

"Yeh, pretty sweet. And yes, I saw them. It was over quickly though, they just cut through me and took the briefcase. Left me on the damned grass, buzzing."

"Ouch! Well, you'll be fine. We really need to do something about all the Deadheads though, it's getting too much. Normal people are getting hurt. I'm not going near that park again, not alone anyway."

"Me neither. And those martial arts worms, whatever they were, didn't help a bit, I didn't even see the attack coming."

"Waste of money." Sabre offers me another chocolate, I refuse, and she chomps it down. "Anyway I just came to check you're okay. And to give you this in person." She swipes at the window and a Get Well Soon card appears: the staff and some students are smiling, with Doctor Hello at the centre. "I added Hello, I know how much you love and admire him."

"Yeh, thanks for that." I pull a face, part playful and part genuinely disgruntled. "He's my hero."

Sabre doesn't come back to the hospital and the week drags. The thought of going back to the school – to the insipid jargon of Doctor Hello, the sweat-laden staff, the smarmy kids, the hours of boredom, the worms, everything except for Sabre – fills me with jitters, so I take meds to ease my nerves. I spend my wages on printer data, some new games, a few dozen books, put a couple of worms on order, cancel them. I watch the rolling news: crisis in the far West, politicians bickering, education at the centre of most stories.

"The divide between rich and poor," the broadcaster says, "is epidemic." He visits a worm farm, a vast glimmering factory full of flashing glass tanks. He dips his gloved hand into a tank and pulls out a handful of worms, shows how they flinch at bright lights. "It's learned from their ancestors," he says to the camera. We know the story by now, but he tells it anyway. History repeats. "These worms never experienced light and shock therapy, yet they react to it. The reflex memory is passed on through the chemicals of other worms' experiences." The camera cuts to the human labs. "This lab collects data from these great minds." Rows of men and women sit, reading books and data sheets, swiping windows, listening to music through headphones. "All this, to make worms. But some feel that the big question still needs answers: are worms really good for us? Only time will tell."

I turn the news off, pack my bags and stretch the fingers of my new hand. No scars, the kids will be disappointed. I'm a little disappointed, too. Everyone likes a scar, it's a story lived and worth remembering.

Russell Jones is an Edinburgh-based writer and editor. He has published 4 collections of poetry, and has edited 2 poetry anthologies. He is deputy and poetry editor of *Shoreline of Infinity*. Russell also writes YA fiction. He has a PhD in Creative Writing from The University of Edinburgh.

SF Caledonia

Monica Burns

First published in 1874, this book is unmistakeably a work of science fiction. It is Andrew Blair's *Annals of the Twenty-Ninth Century; Or, The Autobiography of the Tenth President of the World Republic*.

In a nutshell, it is a future history of Earth as a conglomerated World Republic that has become a technologically and socially advanced Utopia by the 2800s. It describes the countless inventions, social progress, the ambition and achievement of a society in the prime of its life. And there is even some space travel.

Unfortunately, the book is quite rare, so I could only find Volume 1 to read, but the story goes on for a further two volumes in which the protagonist ventures to Venus and Mars.

Volume 1 is narrated by Diogenes Milton, the tenth president of the World Republic, as he chronicles the years of his own lifetime and their personal, political and scientific landmarks. A considerable portion of the book is spent reflecting on the great advances of his century, in comparison to life in the previous millennium, specifically the 19th century.

I'll admit that I did not initially warm to this book. I was gnashing my teeth at the chapters and chapters of 'info-dumping'. The author's intention, obviously was to fill the readers in on all the events and progress in the time between the 19th century and the 29th, and to wow a contemporary

Victorian audience with the marvels he describes, but it could have been doing with less of that and more in the way of concrete plot. I almost laughed when I saw that a newspaper article from Blair's time, 1885, in the *Dundee Evening Telegraph* made a similar point:

ANNALS OF THE

TWENTY-NINTH CENTURY;

OR,

The Autobiography of the Tenth President of the World-Republic.

IN THREE VOLUMES.
VOL. I.

London:
SAMUEL TINSLEY,
10, SOUTHAMPTON STREET, STRAND.
1874.
[*The right of translation is reserved.*]

"Its fault is in that the first and second volumes the author permitted himself to run into a diffusion of language and an extravagance of imagination that keeps the reader too long from getting at the *raison d'être* of the work."

Modern criticism also picks up on this but readers ultimately, past and present, seem to be forgiving of its flaws in the light of the enormous scope of Blair's imagination. The same article goes on to say that,

"The book, which is characterised by much boldness of thought, is a politico-social satire, and is written in a style at once incisive, trenchant, and brilliant."

The article also tells us that the novel was a hit when it first came out. Apparently it "created little short of a sensation in literary circles" when it was published. The initial lack of narrative is made up for in stunning inventions and colourful and emotive description of the future world. I would say this book is a science fiction artist's dream. It is so densely packed with description of dynamic inventions and extraordinary views of cityscapes, skies, mountains and space, that it would really come to life as a series of pictures around the walls of a gallery.

The amount of inventions and concepts are staggering. I simply will not be able to list them all, but here are my favourite few: mankind has worked out how to control the weather and adjusts it to suit; energy is harvested from volcanoes; there are armies of tamed animals trained to undertake tasks of burden; birds are trained to sing in choirs; and humans each have a pair of metal wings that enable them to fly, and it has become common that people enjoy courting in the sky. A few of Blair's other flights of fancy happen to be uncannily far-seeing and bear remarkable resemblance to the inventions of the digital age: there are microscopic books, enabling the ease of transport of thousands of volumes of literature; there's a system of pneumatic tubes which enable audio broadcasts and objects such as newspapers to be sent immediately to anywhere in the planet, meaning the whole world gets the same news at the same time (completely normal to us in the internet age, but a marvel to Blair in 1874); and there are powerful telescopes that allow someone to see across the world to anywhere they choose, which sounds more or less exactly like satellite imagery.

Blair predicts infinitely optimistic things for mankind, declaring poetically that "Science has confiscated the contents of Pandora's box". He bravely attempts an explanation about *how* the world's evils have been eradicated by science, but occasionally it is brushed aside so carelessly it becomes rather self-parodying - especially when the narrator casually adds that murder is a thing of the past. Although the President Diogenes Milton presents a very positive picture of the world's progress, it reminded me of, in our own world, the way history often relayed to us—the ways in which often a country's national narrative, the stories it tells itself about its own history—are often distorted in order to maintain systems of power and oppression. With a report as positive as this from the President of the World Republic, I couldn't help but wonder what he is smothering beneath the mask of a shining utopia—about who is being repressed and the lies the World Republic is telling itself about its society and the state of the planet in order to convince itself and the people that they are doing the right thing.

It is not a huge leap of the imagination to make these suggestions: there are some elements of the book that hinted to me that not all is as good in the world as Milton suggests. For example, it is decided in the World's Parliament that the mountains of the world are to be levelled to the ground for aesthetic purposes, because they are "scabs on the face of fair nature". Blair often writes poetically, and sometimes poignantly and he does so at this moment, "Thus, amid universal acclimation, it was decreed that the everlasting hills should be everlasting no longer."

Not only are the mountains to be destroyed, but vast swathes of the world seem to have merged into one. There is a moment where Edinburgh is described as "a beautiful district in the city of Britain". To me this picture sounds like a nightmare! A world where Man has so entirely consumed the natural world that there is no countryside left, no mountains left to climb or gaze at, it sounds too scarily like the future we may run headlong into if we're not careful. On top of all that, globalisation has gone to the extremes that there is one centralised government, one religion that everyone follows, zero diversity or nationality. That sounds more like the basis of a dystopia, or a daydream for the small-minded.

In what world could murder no longer exist? Is the justice system so strict that fear keeps the people in check? Or have they cracked their own version of Precrime as in *Minority Report*? Such details don't stand a great deal of digging—unless of course, you are a writer and like to ask yourself *what if* as a spring-board for inspiration, in which case this book is a gold mine.

I realised, while reading this book, that I was a little harsh in judging it. For a modern-day author to include important world-building details with such shaky foundations like this, critics would go right through them—but for a someone writing in the 1870s, someone whose whole life seems to have been contained within a seventy mile radius, it is really rather impressive. When compared to other SF authors we've met in this series, such as James Leslie Mitchell and George MacDonald, writers whose travels to foreign lands must have broadened their horizons and therefore their imaginations, Andrew Blair is not known to have travelled much further afield than his home region of Fife and neighbouring Angus. Considering not only the time period in which he lived, but his exposure to the world on the short time he lived on this planet, he had an incredible imagination. Also, it must be acknowledged that he was only 25 years old when *Annals of the Twenty-Ninth Century* was published. It is not to say that Blair never travelled outwith his home counties, just that his life is not well-documented. Most of the information I managed to scrape together came from the aforementioned article in the *Dundee Evening Telegraph*, announcing the death of a well-known and well-liked young doctor in Tayport.

Blair was born in Dunfermline in 1849, studied Medicine at the University of Edinburgh and from there he went on to become a doctor. He practiced in Coupar-Angus, Ceres and Strathkinnes and finally in Tayport, where he died after eight or nine years of service to the community there. Tragically, he was only 35 years old when he died, leaving behind a wife and one daughter. The *Dundee Evening Telegraph* reports that he caught a severe cold that meant he was confined to his house for months, which ultimately badly affected his lungs and ended his life in the January of 1885.

The article praised his character, his conduct as a doctor and his writing: "In Tayport he was highly esteemed. He was a public-spirited man, and took much interest in all the affairs of the village. [...] He was a most genial and entertaining companion - his conversation being full of jokes, anecdotes, and apt quotations - and as a friend he was generous to a fault." They went on to say he was "a singularly well-informed man of refined literary tastes. He was widely read on many subjects, and being possessed of a powerful memory, he could use his information with telling effect both in conversation and in writing. He was indeed a writer of unusual ability."

Now since moving to Dundee myself, and seeing the modern Tay Bridge every day, with the remains of its predecessor standing as stumps beside it (the original bridge famously collapsed in 1879 during a storm), I can't help but wonder about Andrew Blair. Living in Tayport during this decade, a town under ten miles away and within sight of the bridge, he would have living memories of both its construction and its tragic fall. He was practising in Tayport while its foundations were being laid. I wonder how much this inspired his book—the optimism and excitement surrounding the construction of a new feat of engineering, a record-breaking structure, the longest bridge in the world at the time.

Annals of the Twenty-Ninth Century was published just four or five years before the Tay Bridge Disaster—I would love to know what Blair thought, whether or not it shook his soaring optimism for progress. It seems the anxiety about great disaster accompanying great achievement wasn't absent from his mind, as one of the chapters in *Annals* is titled 'The Great Accident of the Age' and describes how a rogue boulder, during a dismantling of a mountain tumbled down the side of the mountain and crushed a town.

The extract I have chosen reminded me so much of the 1902 silent film by Georges Méliès *Le Voyage Dans la Lun (A Trip to the Moon)*. Yet Blair was voyaging to the moon almost thirty years before this groundbreaking fantasy film.

Just before this extract, Diogenes Milton and his friends (who are, like many of the book's characters, brazenly named for eminent individuals) Shakespeare Socrates and Stephenson Watt have returned from their first botched attempt at reaching the moon. I like this passage for its sense of realism. Blair has put a great deal of thought into imagining what it would be like to travel into space. He is realistic in the limits of the technology and the characters learn from their mistakes and improve the technology for the next venture. Then he describes the enormity of the task, the sublimity of outer-space and the anxieties of space-travellers. Blair has a powerful imagination that doesn't only imagine the spectacle and the fantasy, but ruminates on the physical and psychological implications of in space travel.

It is easy as modern readers to grow bored of scenes that look down on earth from space, but remember Andrew Blair was writing in a time where that view was still 87 years away, and even with his wild imagination he didn't expect it to be possible until the 29th century.

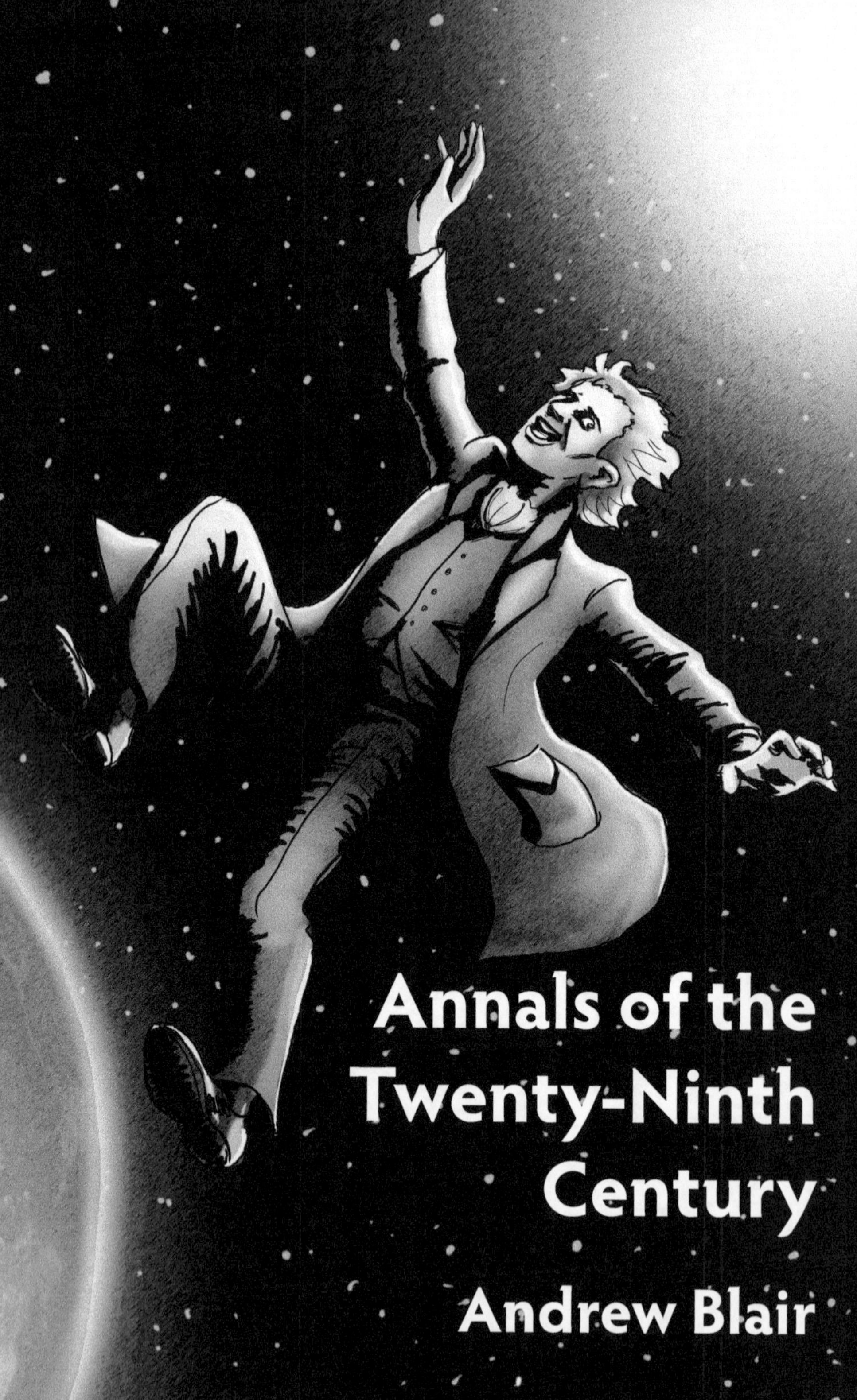

Annals of the Twenty-Ninth Century

Andrew Blair

CHAPTER XVII.

Between Heaven and Earth.

The idea of a journey to the moon was now rescued from the dungeons of scepticism. The hitherto untrodden cantons of ultra-aerial dynamics were soon overrun by the feet of research. Improved altimeters, non-aerial barometers, and thousands of trans-atmospheric apparatus were invented weekly. The mountain tops of success are ever invested by pathless glaciers and precipices. Determined to storm these redoubts, we advanced with hearts garrisoned with the ammunition of courage and perseverance. Accordingly, we prepared to make another expedition into the firmament. We commenced by facturing a more complete ultra-mundane locomotive, which comprised such an amazing concentration of ingenuity and such an aggregation of inventions, such an embodiment of skill, and such an incorporation of volatility and strength, that it took two years to focus these wondrous properties into its workmanship. It was a mechanical marvel. The same size as the last, it was a hundred times more powerful, and it possessed the additional advantage of requiring a crew of only half the number.

The trial trips in this engine extended over six months, during which time we greatly increased its velocity, and introduced into it a large budget of little comforts. The grand but abortive attempt was then made to invade the moon. Our trans-aerial ship was not only stocked with the most nutritive food, but a new idea was adopted, in supplying each of its mariners with physiological antitriptic apparatus. Such was their excellence, that a few grammes of food and a table-spoonful of water daily were rendered quite sufficient for the maintenance of life. The other arrangements were so consummately ingenious, that we verily believed we would be enabled to cross the mundo-lunar gulf. Our effort was sublime in its boldness. Perhaps our band might never again see earth. Sacrifices on the altar of scientific research, we might be wafted like meteoric stones upon some other world. Our bones might not return to the dust whence they came, but be revolved for an infinity of time in an infinity of space. The thought could not but make us turn our eyes to our Father in heaven, bold in the assurance that though our remains might be waifs in the universe for thousands of ages, we would still be supported by His gracious hand. Even if martyrs, we were dying for the greatest cause of this great age. When, in the past, men went to the field of slaughter to murder or be murdered, merely on account of the silly squabbles of kings as to what kind of flag should flutter over a certain piece of ground, could we grudge to risk our lives for the noblest of projects in this the era of cosmopolitanism, the epoch of the millennium?

Our crew, consisting of Copernicus Galileo, Stephenson Watt, Caxton Arkwright, Shakespeare Socrates, and myself, left our terrestrial home amid the benedictions of our fellow-men. Millions had come from every quarter of the world to view the great ascension, and the scene and services merited their assemblage. The very circumstance that it was Mount Ararat from which our Hegira to the moon took place, lent a sacredness to the solemnities. Where the ark had first rested we were now about to embark in another ark, in which we were to seek another Ararat in another world. Henry Bunyan, who conducted the services, spoke with an inspiration which have endowed his words into the classics. Millions on the Mount and in the air, by means of their auroscopes, heard his molten language; and never did ears listen to a more impressive discourse, or eyes witness such an impressive sight. At length our balloon weighed anchor. A procession of ten hundred thousand aerial mariners escorted us to the suburbs of the atmosphere, anthems being played the while with such beauty, as swathed our souls in a halo of heavenly joy. Arrived at the shores of the air, we left the great sight and the triumphant sounds behind us, and launched into the dark gloomy trans-aerial ocean. For a while our eyes and hearts wandered back to our friends, but our duty soon urged us to direct our eyes upwards, and centre our resolutions in winning the moon. Our speed was equally pleasing to ourselves and our brethren on the earth. With natural delight we saw terrestial objects exact a small and still smaller dividend of our retinae. Every incident omened well. The non-aerial breathing machine, the acoustical devices, and the log-lines, worked with success, while our spirits were buoyed up with the most cheerful expectations. At mid-day we had our first meal, according to the antitriptic system. Two and a half kilogrammes of food sufficed us all, yet each of us had enough to satisfy his requirements. Not since the multitudes had fed on the loaves and fishes did ever any company have their appetites slaked with so small a proportion of viands. Chameleon-like, we might have almost have been said to have lived on air. But the mere skeleton of a summary must suffice for the log-book of the trans-terrestrial voyage. In the first week we journeyed 1,100 kilometres daily on an average, during which time we observed four undiscovered moonules. In the second week, in consequence of being nearer the moon, and having a greater share of its gravitation and less of that of the world, we averaged 1,300 kilometres daily. In the third week we increased this to 1,600, in the fifth to 2,000, in the sixth to 2,600, and in the seventh to the amazing velocity of 3,500 kilometres daily. Up to this point we surmounted every difficulty, though all the while deeply alive to the peril of our position and the wildness of our adventure. Now we had collisions with meteors, anon we were drifted out of our course by a constellation of moonules. Nestled in mid-air, 80,000 miles from a world, we lived in regions in which there was no air to breathe, no food to eat, and no water to drink. Though the physiological plans which enabled us to breathe where there was no atmosphere, and to fast without suffering starvation, were akin to perfection, our eyes longed to view the fair face of our mother earth —our mouths watered to taste its fruits, and even our souls thirsted to feel the enjoyments of home. Coffined within a small car, we felt as if we lived without feeling life. Beyond the scenes and influences of humanity, our very senses were famished. The appetites of sight, smell, touch, taste, and hearing, each suffered a dearth. While our mind's machinery was in full play, our physical feelings seemed exiled from their true spheres. A small balloon was our world, wherein our ears only heard the sound of our own voices, and our eyes viewed the awful sight of a double firmament with its zenith and nadir.

Heaven to us was not a canopy, but a great rotund vault, of which we were the centre—a vault marvellously bespangled with star brilliants, and a vault whose milky way was a silverway, and zodiacal light an aurora. Half the day we looked down upon the sun. Day and night a firmament with myriads of stars lay beneath our feet. Alone in the trackless tracts of immensity we saw our native world dwindled into a moon. We were in regions concurrently cheered by sun-light, moon-light, world-light, and star-light. What appearances could have been more reverence-inspiring than those we viewed? Could the wildest of Dantes, Miltons, or Coleridges, have supposed anything more wonder-fraught than a miniature world of a few metres in diameter, with a population of only five inhabitants, and in possession of a firmament containing two moons to which in size ours was a dwarf and in lambency a rush-light—a firmament not of 190°, but 380°, in which a sun, two moons, the milky way, the zodiacal light, and a complete muster of the stellar hosts, shone simultaneously, undimmed by the medium of any atmosphere ? Yet truth, which so out-fictions fiction, rendered these wonders realities. Above our small entity of worlddom was the earth-like moon, below was the moon-like earth, and all around the glorious unclouded stellorama of infinity. What conditions could arouse more intense feelings or excite more sublime ideas ? Even the writings we composed in those vacuous

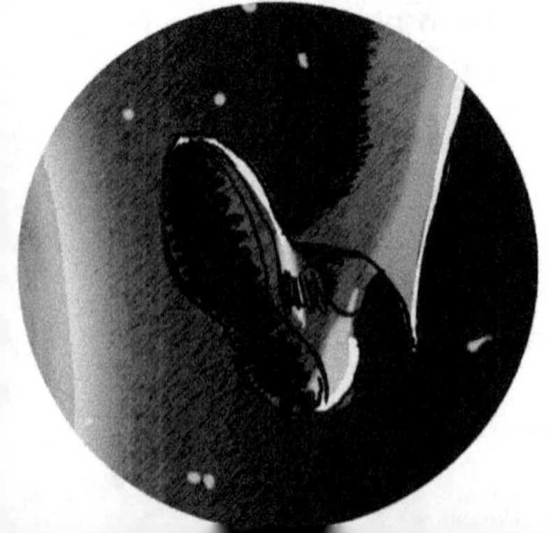

realms breathe a religious fervour, nobility of sentiment, and earnest glowing eloquence, equalled in none of our earthly works. Could any circumstances so estrange us from the sordidness of the world as the possibility that we might never return to it in the body ? Never was such a sermon vouchsafed us on the littleness of man, and his utter dependence upon Providence. Those who have never left the fire-side of the earth cannot appreciate the numberless bounties which rain unconsciously upon them during every throb of their pulse; but we who were removed from its scenes were enabled to see them by the powerful telescope of their absence.

But I am brought to the straits to which we were driven after having lived eight weeks upon the unnatural method essential for territories without food, air, land, or water. Our strength began to fail and our courage to be damped, so that we were outflanked, and forced back to the conviction that science was still unable to cope with the multitudes of exigencies which such a journey as ours entailed. Nevertheless, we held out for another week, feeding our fortitude on our moonward ambition. Our speed during this time was four times that at our outset. On this account we stood exactly half-way between the earth and its consort on the sixtieth day of our extraterrestrial exile. Each day had seen these two visually great, but astronomically small, orbs changing, the moon growing larger and larger, the earth smaller and smaller, both merging from their gradations, of new to full moon and full to new moon, new to full earth and full to new earth. Having proceeded so far, we again tried to blow up the  embers of our determination. Our hearts being magnetic towards moonland, we strove on three days longer, when, to our unutterable grief, Galileo took seriously ill. The rest of us being far from well, we were forced amid heart-rending regrets to behold the death of our cherished hopes, and to take a longing look at the moon, after having journeyed towards it more than half-way. We then relaxed our dietetic system, halted our aerial chariot, and made a few final investigations before sounding our retreat. Applying our scales, we found the force of gravitation so small that our balloon only weighed a few pounds and ourselves a few ounces. We next threw a few small articles out of our bark, and found they only fell a few inches in a minute. Interested in a tenet which science had so long held, but which the senses had never before witnessed, I boldly jumped out of the balloon into the great abyss of Vacuity. Unnatural though it seemed, I fell not, but then I was standing on nothing. Like Peter, my faith led me to walk on an unwonted element, but, like him, my valiantness soon melted. Though at first delighted with the singular sensation of being suspended in a vacuum, I became terrified when I looked down, and still more when, in my absence of mind, trying to advance towards my aerial vessel, I saw all my exertions brought me not nearer it one iota. I had forgotten, indeed, in leaping out, that the element in which I had ventured was not one in which I could swim. My friends laughed heartily at my needless anxiety, and to comfort me Stephenson Watt leaped out and bore me company, while he, at the same time, handed me a rope with which we were enabled to re-enter our craft. After a few further experiments and investigations, night came on, and night though it was, we at once shaped our course to the earth. We erringly thought we should not err by trusting only to our instruments. The action of the engines, joined to the increased force of gravitation, made us dart down with a velocity at which speed itself might have been startled. Every moment our momentum increased, but as there was no atmosphere to clog our inertia or to make us feel that when falling we were falling, we had only the sensation of being stationary, while the world was a huge ball advancing upward, and the moon another in full retreat. Such was our composure, that we failed to take the precautions which were so necessary—we failed to note how quickly the world was becoming world-like and the moon moon-like. Shakespeare Socrates and Stephenson Watt were busily engaged in completing some investigations; Caxton Arkwright was studying the action of our bark's machinery; while I was employed in nursing our sick brother Copernicus Galileo. Our speed, moreover, was so much beyond our calculation, that we were startled when daylight dawned four hours afterwards, and showed us the earth at a distance of only a few hundred miles. It was now too late to reverse our engines, and apply the ultra-aerial drag to impede our impetuous impetus. With the energy of despair, however, we strove to lessen our danger, but, short of a miracle, nothing could enable us to escape, and a miracle not being forthcoming, we crashed against the atmosphere with such suddenness and violence, as kindly bathed us in the sweet waters of insensibility. Happily, those on earth had noticed our Icarus-like fall, and had prepared a suitable arrangement to save us from serious injury. Despite this, the concussion was so great, that each of us, Vulcan-like, had our legs broken. Such was the suddenness of the accident, and such the wild overthrow of our senses, that our ship was wrecked ere we had time to realise we were near the world. Our ultra-aerial equipments were undoffed, for, in our stupor, we knew not the moment when we had entered the atmosphere. As for our wounds, it was only the case of Galileo that gave us any concern, on account of his previous indisposition. Happily he, as well as the remainder of us, rallied so quickly that our misfortunes did not vex us so much as the damage to our balloon and our instruments. A few days' hygiene repaired our tabernacles, but it took weeks to refit our mutilated locomotive. The accident, as being the only one which had happened in the world since the Matterhorn catastrophe, was deeply deplored; but it could not daunt the irrepressible energies of man to make renewed sorties to the moon. Our mission, notwithstanding its failure, had reaped a rich harvest of scientific discoveries, and glowed with the omens of future success. The composition of the trans-aerial ether, its electrical peculiarities, the countless shoals of meteoric with which it abounded, its peculiarities at different altitudes and under diverse conditions, had not only been investigated, but their phenomena completely unveiled. We had likewise proved the possibility of man living for weeks and even months by artificial physiological adaptations in the regions of vacuity.

Interview: Stephen Palmer

From his debut 20 years ago with Memory Seed, Stephen Palmer has become one of the most individual voices in British science fiction and fantasy.

Here he talks to Gary Dalkin about his recent work, including his new Young Adult *Factory Girl* trilogy.

Gary Dalkin: Your new trilogy, which I haven't had an opportunity to read yet, is YA. Before that, your most recent books, *Beautiful Intelligence* and its sequel *No Grave For A Fox* are near-future hard science fiction set in same universe as *Muezzinland*. They are particularly appealing in that they strive to present as much as possible a global vision, spanning different cultures and continents, and all levels of society, from homeless street musicians in Fez to the five star world of the super rich. Is this kind of hard SF something you plan to write more of? Will there be further additions to the *Beautiful Intelligence* series?

Stephen Palmer: I think it's unlikely that I will return to the *Beautiful Intelligence* world; events in genre fiction would have to spin out of control for that to happen. I'm the sort of author who follows his muse, which usually means artistic satisfaction and relatively little commercial success. Not that I'm in this for the money, you understand! As for the inclusion of what might be termed the 'lower levels' of society into my work, I've always been drawn to 'outsider' characters and issues, being myself very much a fish out of water in British, conservative, technophilic, capitalist society. Alas, 'ordinary' people in modern Britain really are outsiders, since the ruling elite serves only itself, including through the ballot box. Though I can come across sometimes as a rabid Lefty, I'm really much more of a Green Liberal—the ultimate political outsiders in Britain.

Then there's the whole Africa thing. That started out as a love of the music, but it's broadened to a fascination with the land and its cultures, especially North and West Africa. I bought a kora last year (the West African twenty-one string harp) which I'm hoping to learn to play. A beautiful musical instrument. My sympathies lie very much with 'ordinary' people who have 'ordinary' lives being shafted by the semi-insane men who rule them. I'm anti-Tory, anti-religion, anti-royal, anti-patriarchy; in other words, pro-human. I was recently described by one reviewer as having a tendency to didacticism, but I think that comes more from having a social conscience than anything else.

YA fiction for me isn't a new thing—I've got a few unpublished YA novels stacked away on the Mac—but I am beginning to see it as a valuable route to a new way of writing. I hope my readers warm to this new route. Besides, as Philip Pullman's outstanding *His Dark Materials* illustrates, you can write a YA novel with adult themes. My new work—the *Factory Girl* trilogy; *The Girl With Two Souls / The Girl With One Friend / The Girl With No Soul*—is not dissimilar, being an alternate-world Edwardian adventure whose underlying theme is the nature of the human condition, and particularly the question of whether or not human beings have a soul.

I can definitely see me writing more YA novels. A lot of my work involves people making discoveries about the world they live in—Zinina and Arrahaquen in *Memory Seed*, Dwllis in *Glass*, Psolilai and psolilai in *Urbis Morpheos*—and the YA novel, with its relatively naïve characters, is one great way to follow that theme of discovery.

GD: I'm intrigued to know what you mean by describing yourself as being 'anti-religion', yet in the same answer going on you reveal you've just written three novels about whether or not human beings have a soul. Aren't matters of the soul, whether you believe we have one or not, the very heart of religion?

SP: First of all I'd better say that I'm an atheist, and, for various reasons, I find myself opposed not only to the great majority of the core ideas of religion, but also to it as a monolithic patriarchal structure—the cause of suffering, grief, violence, intolerance and incalculable horror over the last five thousand years. But I'd also like to quote one of my characters in *The Girl With One Friend*: "All I say to you is this. Individual people of faith are not to be mocked, as he mocked you. But the religion itself… that is fair game." Thirdly, I'd like to mention that the friend in my own life who I've known for the longest time, who's been a close friend and colleague for decades, is a Christian, and I'm fine with that. We've had some good and useful conversations;

plus, he's a really great bloke. Finally, I'd like to add that a small proportion of the core values of some religions—notably the Golden Rule; do unto others as you would have them do unto you—are valuable and worth placing into humane ethics.

Having said all that… religion is at its heart anti-understanding. It's a prehistoric hang-over from times when all human beings grasped the world through self-centred structures: magic, spiritualism, animism and so on. All these structures were built up in geographically localised, often tribal zones, but they had an absolutely crucial function in prehistoric times: they allowed one fundamental part of the human condition to have its essential expression—the drive to explain and comprehend the world. This in my view is one of those parts of the human condition that, however warm and fluffy you feel about animals, separates us with an abyss from non-conscious creatures. We make models of the world in our minds: animals essentially use instinct. It is the quality, authenticity and lack of self-centredness of a person's mental model that contributes in overwhelming measure to their character.

In my new trilogy, although the focus is on the characters,

the plot and the story, the underlying theme is these fundamental parts of the human condition. I explore that both through the characters and through an 'alternate' version of *Alice In Wonderland*, which in my tale is by the Rev. Carolus Dodgson and is called Amy's Garden.

I expect religious or 'spiritual' people to be as sceptical of my atheism as I am of their faith. The thing is; they never are. So, regarding the latter part of the question: in my opinion, the single most important task of humanity now is to develop a scientific description of the human condition. We have done pretty well so far, considering that the game-changer—Freud's discovery of the unconscious— only occurred about a century ago. I think that, without a description linking the nature of consciousness as created by evolution by natural selection with the actualities of the human condition which we all experience—love, emotion, a sense of passing time, the comprehension of death, a meaning-framework, creativity, identity etc—we can't understand what's happening around us in human societies: capitalism, communism, patriarchy, organised religion, terrorism, authoritarianism… the list is almost endless. So

the question of the likelihood of human souls is not only a relevant query for atheists to consider, it's an essential one, since all prehistoric spiritualism and all modern religions posit some sort of soul/spirit—and that fact has to be explained in any full description of the human condition.

I can't myself seriously consider any kind of soul or spirit for individuals, in fact I personally think it's one of the most dangerous prehistoric ideas still with us. The irony is, it was absolutely inevitable that the notion would dig itself deep into the human psyche because of the impossibility of considering the reality of death from a prehistoric perspective. I've tried to consider this question from both sides in my trilogy.

GD: It's interesting that you'd say, "religion is at its heart anti-understanding…" There's a contradiction in saying religion is anti-understanding, then that religion comes out of the drive to explain and comprehend the world. If religion is a 'hang-over' from prehistoric times which still thrives today doesn't that suggest it meets something fundamental in human nature which isn't answered elsewhere? As Juanita says in Neil Stephenson's *Snow Crash* –

"All people have religions. It's like we have religion

receptors built into our brain cells ..."

In which case an interesting question would be, why? And another would be, how do we respond?

If I were to be sceptical of your atheism I would be doubting your sincerity, which would not just be offensive, but fly in the face of the evidence. The evidence being that you are an atheist, because you tell me that you are, and that I've no reason to doubt you're telling the truth. That might be why people are never sceptical of your atheism. Which is obviously different to being sceptical about atheism itself...

SP: Oops, yes, points of semantics—I meant understanding as in non-guesswork understanding. As you say, the drive to find meaning is entirely rooted in the human condition; in our use of mental models. It's fundamental to who we are as a species. The big difference is: faith explicitly rejects the idea of testing the real world, while the scientific method does test the real world. By 'my atheism' I meant atheism.

Your *Snow Crash* quote is an excellent example of what we're discussing. I don't think there are 'religious receptors' in our brains, that's an inappropriate analogy, since receptors work in massively parallel arrays—

tens, hundreds of billions of them. But every one of us is undoubtedly hard-wired to develop and use a meaning-framework, of which of course atheism is one of many. The 'why' of this is because of the human mind's use of a mental model. Without meaning there is no coherence, and without coherence there is insanity.

GD: Without going too much further down this path, which is straying a long way from any direction discussion of your books! I'm intrigued that you say we're undoubtedly hard-wired to use a meaning-framework, the niggling question obviously being, why? I mean, how do you resolve the apparent paradox that a lack of meaning results in insanity when—and I'm presuming this here, so correct me if I'm wrong—as an atheist you would consider the universe the result of chance, rather than meaningful action? Where does a need for meaning so important that without it insanity ensues come from in such a universe, in which the very idea of meaning itself must be meaningless? Not only shouldn't meaning be necessary to underpin the coherence which supports sanity, it shouldn't even exist.

Apart from which, faith doesn't explicitly reject testing the real world, though some 'faiths' may do so. All the time we accept things 'on faith' based on observational evidence—I see white stuff falling from the sky so I believe that it is snowing without going outside to test that what is falling really is snow. Equally I don't run tests to try and work out if I am in some virtual reality being fed a simulation of something I think of as snow. That would be self-defeating as we can never get beyond the evidence of our own senses.

And ultimately none of us can prove all our assumptions. There comes a point when everyone takes what they believe on 'faith'—I've not seen God, though I'm aware of plenty of evidence which can rationally and coherently be pointed in the direction of a creator—the same as I've not seen a sub-atomic particle but believe they exist because it's rational to infer their existence from various indirect effects.

SP: When you see white stuff falling from the sky, you don't need to do any testing—it's an already proven event. Snow isn't taken on faith, just as the existence of the Earth and the Moon aren't taken on faith. (You'd need to be a solipsist to bother with all that.) So, snow isn't something you need to make any effort to believe in— belief not required. Similarly, you don't need to believe in Newtonian mechanics, nor keep doing experiments to test it. It's the law.

I do agree with you that, at the extremes of both sides of this discussion, neither the atheist nor the believer can prove their position. But that rather sidesteps the point that science says "beyond reasonable doubt," eg. it is beyond reasonable doubt that frozen water falls from the sky as snow. We don't need to keep doing experiments to show that it does happen in the real, testable world.

To return to the main question: *We're undoubtedly hard-wired… it shouldn't even exist.*

I don't think there is a paradox in the existence of a random, chance-driven physical world containing conscious beings having an absolute requirement for those conscious beings to use meaning frameworks. One thinks of the oft-repeated position of religion trying to claim that only faith-based frameworks based in books written millennia ago can explain this fundamental drive, as if, because we now live in a world explained by science, we are being told to live our human lives according to science—not humanity. That argument should I think be seen as the fraudulent sleight-of-hand it is. But as a species we have yet to create what above I called "the single most important task of humanity now… to develop a scientific description of the human condition." The point that I think is most often missed (or more likely ignored, since the majority of philosophers are men) is that human beings evolved into conscious creatures in *societies*. As Dirk Ngma says in *Beautiful Intelligence*: "I think consciousness [is] between people, not in a brain. It [is] *between* us all, like water for fish." A single, isolated baby who had their every physical need cared for would not in my opinion become conscious as it grew up, because consciousness can only exist in a society of human beings all of whom have that potential. It is an emergent property. Consequentially, so is the need for meaning emergent, not to mention all the other aspects of the human condition.

For 13.8 billion years the universe evolved according to those laws and initial conditions that epitomised it. Then we came along. Quite possibly conscious beings have already evolved on other planets; they will have faced the same questions we do. But on Earth, the arrival of conscious human beings did not alter the random, physical law-driven universe (at least, not on the macroscopic scale—but quantum mechanics may have something to say elsewhere…).

The meaning of our lives comes from ourselves, not from any external agency. This is why I keep emphasising the need for a scientific description of the human condition. The time has come to discard imaginary descriptions and to determine what in the human condition makes us crave meaning. To paraphrase Carl Sagan: the long childhood of humanity is over.

If I could quote a brief passage from *The Girl With One Friend*:

> "Sir George stood up, his knees creaking, but Erasmus caught him by the sleeve. 'What shall I say when he asks me what is to replace Christianity? I cannot say science.'

> "Sir George glanced at Kora. 'Why not describe the simple human dignity of your friendship with Kora?' "

We also shouldn't forget the importance of the fact that consciousness evolved according to the rules of natural selection. It must therefore have a profoundly important reason for having emerged— an observation made with most brilliance by Nicholas Humphrey in his ground-breaking book *The Inner Eye*. Had consciousness emerged in groups of proto-humans but led to insanity owing to fundamental differences in its qualities, those groups would have been selected against, and their offspring would have disappeared. But *we* didn't disappear. We really are all one.

GD: That's all genuinely fascinating and we could discuss this endlessly, though I'm aware this is already becoming a long interview so perhaps we should return to your books. In an interview with Tony Ballantyne you said "I have a feeling that [the *Factory Girl* trilogy] could be an important point in my development as an author." Did you mean in terms of the quality of the books, their potential for commercial success, the subject matter or style, some combination of all of these, or something else entirely?

SP: Definitely the commercial angle, but also a kind of awareness (still a little undefined in my mind) that I've somehow put my overtly experimental novels behind me and come up with something that feels more traditional. I did a final edit of the trilogy before sending it off to Keith Brooke, and the word that I unexpectedly used to describe it all when I mentioned it on the phone to a friend was 'epic'— even though it's mostly set in the Sheffield of 1910-11. I don't know… I just have a feeling that this one is different in some way.

That's not to say I won't ever experiment again. I believe in it, I believe in giving my fans something entirely unexpected, I believe in stretching myself as a writer, and I do believe (though it's often commercial suicide) in writing books that challenge the reader. All the great books I love have this aspect of being challenging— like Gene Wolfe's *The Book Of The New Sun*. If your reader has to invest a lot of themselves into a work, that makes a different kind of relationship than with a read-once-only type of novel. I can definitely see myself writing more YA novels anyway.

Stephen Palmer's latest work is a Young Adult trilogy, *The Girl With Two Souls* (published 22 November), *The Girl With One Friend* (29 November) and *The Girl With No Soul* (6 December).

A fourth volume, *The Conscientious Objector*, set four years later, will follow in spring 2017.

All four books are published by Infinity Plus.

Noise and Sparks 3: Interlude

Ruth EJ Booth

Through the library turnstiles and out into late afternoon. I slip cozy earbuds in and pull down my hat, but hold off pressing play, just let them sit there; a sign to myself as much as anyone else that I'm not to be disturbed. Tenement streets open either side of me, golden halls in the late afternoon light, leaves mouldering to a soft carpet underneath my boots. Sun cracks through rolling cloud. Across the valley, the hills glow red: a gift of a moment. None of this will last.

I feel that strongly here, now. Here, in this place, just a little to the north and west of my hometown, the collapse from mid-October into the depths of Winter is vertiginous; this drop into darkness, accelerated by the same quirk of planetary tilt that brings this land its glorious never-ending Summer evenings, now limned with frost and new possibility. The moments I've had to take stock have been rare, filled with books, events, seminars, deadlines, and an illness covering that sharp tip from indian summer into the long fall. Now I'm no longer confined to bed—no longer cushioned from the threat of looming deadlines—I'm struck by the realization of how much time has moved on without me.

I shouldn't feel this
disorientated. Writing is forever
anchoring yourself to a future
that is almost here—whether
working to deadlines or
seasonal publications, or within
your own distant worlds. So,
while this is the season of mists
and mellow fruitfulness, it's also
the season of frost and snow,
new flowers and March dew,
endless July light. Being a writer
involves living with this seasonal
dissonance as a constant
companion.

But in this new city,
where the seasonal shift has
a difference nuance to the
one I'm used to, missing that deft wrist flick from one to the other
is unsettling. Already nighttime streets run thick with lamplight,
pooling away into drains as I hide under my soaking hoodie.
Already, the morning light is the white hue of a North-East winter
afternoon. Already, the moon is high near midday, accompaniment
to the chill that even now scrapes its fingers through the sun-
drenched air, the first sign of a subtle paring of reality that will be
long under way by the time you read this. I mourn every passing
moment with quiet anxiety. The Orionid Meteor shower snuck up
on me this year without me even realizing it. I should be thinking of
Christmas by now. This gold slope down to the leafy Kelvin will be
all ice by then.

Perhaps this is why this time of year is so rich with stories, not
just the temptation to avoid the cold by getting toasty by the fire.
There's a gothic wonder about it, of the world transformed. In
its atmosphere, the whip and force of winter wind, the peculiar
electricity of a November sky. In the familiar transmuted by snow
into rough shapes of potential—a car-ish something, a tree-ish
something. And more, as the year nears its end, and the dark closes
in. Beyond the fairy lights and tinsel, outside, the sense of the world
thinning, perceptibly, just beyond the glass.

Christmas is the time we feel this the most, something beyond
seasonal dissonance, a kind of spiritual and temporal transparency.
Our present thoughts, rich with memories of Christmas past, are

at once full of the future—the new year, and this year's end. The season resonates with echoes, reflected in tradition and tale and all our giddy expectations of the time of year. Christmas is never Christmas on its own.

The year holds its breath, takes stock. Just short days later, on those nights where the skies open clear above us, the pavements their mirror in crisp December frost, we'll stand and toast in mugs of hot mulled stuff to this glorious All-Time. This is a profoundly science fictional moment, to consider all of time and space and where we stand in it. Who we are. How far we've come this year. What we've achieved. Who couldn't help but find that awesome, inspirational. Utterly fucking terrifying.

Every year it comes around a little faster. Perhaps this is why we make resolutions for the coming year—to set down anchors as security, promises to ourselves that, despite it all, next year will be better. As if we could ever know. All these things that must be done, resolutions, commitments, deadlines, unravel as time races away with us, leaving us in the same cold predicament year after year.

I shiver beneath bare branches in the narrow streets by the river. The feet of the white houses are buried in brown leaves; more, already skeletal and slippery, muddy the gutters. I think of nothing but how little is left of the year. Of how much I could have done, if I only I hadn't been ill. How I'll never make up the time, never catch up. Always feel behind. Never feel settled in this place. My grand plans drift away like leaves.

I pull my scarf closer around my neck, but chill air reaches for the remnants of my cold, catches my breath. I cough, cough again, hard. My breath clouds like mist in front of me.

Breathe.

Breathe in and cough, hack wet and rasping and sore, lungs grating against their insides.

Breathe. Savour the softness of the last balsam tissue against your sore nose. Curse the rough paper of the library toilets.

Breathe. Remember the party. Mulled wine, hot and heady, spilling off a metal spoon. Drops of pulp spilling, squeezed from orange shells bobbing in the ruddy black. The feeling of warmth in your chest.

Breathe the taste of poetry, words, their fat vowels rolling in your mouth. Savour every sensation, every moment. A wooden globe filled with a world of drinks. Butterfly people, transformed by glitter and music. Being read to sleep by terrifying stories. Celebrate it as it passes. The arms of friends. The smell of hot spiced chai. How good it felt to just be there.

Breathe, and wonder when it all changed, the imperceptible click in your mind. Was it when your pen dropped in the middle of class, and you were too focused on the question to notice? The first time you plucked up the courage to talk to a visiting speaker? The invite you didn't expect? The first time you went out by yourself. The first time the flat door locked behind you, and you were all alone there, and that was okay.

Breathe. The last stretch before home slopes down gently across the bridge, the river wide, from side to side. Nearly home. I wonder, when you read this, whether you'll be smiling or crying.

Tonight, the skies will fill with meteors and the night will be aflame. I think of milky way pavements, kick leaves that fly like golden stars.

Ruth Booth is a BSFA award-winning author and student living in Glasgow. Her stories and poetry can be found at **www.ruthbooth.com**

Reviews

The Augur's Gambit / The King's Justice
Stephen Donaldson
Gollancz, 192 / 128 pages
Review: Chris Heyman

To describe a creative project as a palette cleanser would seem to disparage it but there is no more fitting term for *The Augur's Gambit and The King's Justice*, shipped as one volume in America but released in the UK as two individual novellas. Over the last four decades Stephen Donaldson has focussed on several multi-volume series, but in a recent gap between epics he has delivered these twin tales that both follow magicians saving their kingdoms. Donaldson uses his gift for rounded characterisation to distinguish these leads, with one protagonist wide eyed and earnest while the other is a jaded husk.

When Stephen King interrupted a run of cocaine epics with his Different Seasons novellas he included winking confirmation that the four disparate stories had a common setting. Donaldson's tales do not share any hints of co-existence, and this decision works to his advantage. By investing in fresh world building he is able to keep the reader intrigued as the local rules of magic are drip fed on a need to know basis, raising as many questions as they answer. These answers do come, with endings that neatly resolve conflicts that could support much longer books. In interviews Donaldson is keen to play this potential down, positioning himself as an 'efficient' writer, where the universe is created to serve the characters, rather than being planned in great detail beforehand. If the character's story is over, so too is their world.

One such character is Mayhew Gordian of *The Augur's Gambit*. As the Queen's Hieronimer he is a sheltered innocent up to his elbows in dead poultry, looking for the future in the entrails. He's an odd duck, devoted to his queen and her plucky daughter, Excrucia. The Queen is an assertive and inscrutable presence, using a blinkered Mayhew for her own schemes but ultimately he must find his own path and succeed or fail in the trying. With the Queendom of Indemnie foretold to collapse, Mayhew must learn fast to save his country, with the added obstacle that his particular set of skills can't tell him the nature of the threat. This leads to a collaboration with the princess to discover the secret of the island community's mysterious origins. Even as Mayhew's horizons grow we are never allowed to forget how unpleasant his day job is. This grit is moderate by Donaldson's extreme standards. His early Thomas Covenant novels took a delight in repulsing the reader from the protagonist and, however weird, Mayhew is consistently sympathetic.

The concision of these stories means a lack of space for supporting characters, but the few we get do make an impression. There is a particularly fun scheming Baron, coming across like a British character actor doing a Hollywood baddie, at least in my head.

The King's Justice is the leaner novella, and sparks a little less for it. A grizzled old veteran on one last mission is not an original idea but Coriolus Blackened (Just 'Black' to you and me) is an interesting enough presence to spend some time snuffing out ne'er do wells with. Suffering from an old war wound of literal holes in the soul, we soon gather that Black is a fairly moral character; a killer he may be but he still finds the time to help out the odd widower in need. Unfortunately this time Black is out of his depth, a spate of lungs and livers torn from corpses portend to a new and powerful magical opponent. There are less rounded female characters here than in the sister tome, with the limited word count meaning that only Black gets fully developed. It's this brevity that is the story's downfall, with a cracking setup resolved far too quickly.

Of the two stories, *The Augur's Gambit* functions more as a mystery, with Mayhew's naivety accounting for the reader's lack of information. *The King's Justice* has less narrative logic for such a contrivance, though we do meet Black as he enters a town of unsuspecting villagers. This pushes the reader away from the protagonist, emphasising our distance from Black's gloomy mission. It is only when Black takes on the case of a murdered child that we realise he is the hero that these people need, give or take a little grave bothering.

In both books the people and places burn bright and fast, aided by a film of blood, filth and corpses that attract and repulse in equal measure. But it's the stronger *The Augur's Gambit* that will linger for longer after reading, and is one world I'm disappointed Donaldson has left behind so quickly.

Thirty Years of Rain
Neil Williamson, Elaine Gallagher, Cameron Johnston (editors)
Lulu Press, 248 pages
Review: Chris Kelso

There's an old saying that suggests us Scots have more words for rain than an Eskimo does for snow. Despite our majority's staunchly socialist attitudes and trademark pragmatism, for some reason, Scotland has proved fertile ground for the science fiction community, and for writers in general.

Perhaps it has something to do with escapism? Maybe we're all communal dreamers in a post-industrial reverie? Or, perhaps it has more to do with the dreichness that hangs over us in omnipresence, with all that brutalist architecture set in gunmetal grey? We're living the exotic vicariously, you and I.

When it comes to the proliferation of great SF writing, Glasgow in particular remains curiously unparalleled; this is, in no small part, down to the Glasgow Science Fiction Writers Circle—a writers group with a long and prestigious reputation, a refuge for escapists, forged in earnest, and one which has cemented itself as something of an institution since its inauguration thirty years ago. The writers group is also responsible, in part, for the meteoric rise of writers like Louise Welsh, Hal Duncan, Michael Cobley and Phil Raynes

This brings us to *Thirty Years of Rain* – an anthology edited by Neil Williamson, Elaine Gallagher and Cameron Johnston showcasing some of the myriad talent from the GSFWC. The final product is a stunning achievement, a future artefact for later generations to cherish. This book is a gift.

Most of the GSFWC's yield are

well-represented here. There are stories from newer writers, like Heather Valentine and Kenneth Kelly, to established luminaries of Scottish SF, like Hal Duncan and Gary Gibson (including an informative introduction by Duncan Lunan who was, of course, present during the embryonic stages of the Circle).Our maiden voyage is a story by TJ Berg, one of my personal favourites. *The Freedom of Above* offers a fascinating meditation on grief. We focus on a man, Alex, who has recently lost his wife, but thanks to a 3D scanner and other cutting edge facilities that are available, Alex obtains a realistic flesh model of her. The tone is dark, a real mood setter, and Berg ruminates about the complicated stages of losing someone you love.

Also worth special mention early on is Ruth Booth's poem *Picture, of a Winter Afternoon* which only serves to further highlight her inevitable, imminent success. Thoughtful and masterfully written, everyone should sample Booth's brand of melancholy.

There are gems hidden amongst the shorter works here too—TW Moses's Purge-esque metaphor for keyboard warriors is brilliant, Ian Hunter's witty list of things to know about staple-removers will have you chuckling, and Jim Campbell's flash fiction piece which details one man's quest through a suburban wilderness to find the illusive "Amanda". These are just a few examples.

Another one of my favourites, Fergus Bannon's *The Unusual Genitals Party* is about a group of university students who hold a twisted soiree and offer prize money to, yes, you've guessed it, the most unusual genitals on display. Bannon's prose is exquisitely seedy and the story's slow-build and concurrent climax (excuse the pun) is deliciously droll in its execution, more than you'd imagine might be present in a story so titled. Bannon is another writer teetering on the ergosphere of greatness. Definitely check him out.

Hal Duncan's story is also an absolute cracker as well, but then this is a writer who has a long affiliation with the group. Hal is one of the group's golden sons, profane and eloquent in equal measure, a self-dubbed enfant terrible. *Ascending* manages to evoke the experimental typography of Ginsberg, play around with Moorcock's punk aesthetic and bask in Samuel Delaney's deviancy, while still retaining Hal's 'Hal-ness'. A brilliant centrepiece to the book and a nice wee vignette from his Scruffian saga too.

One common theme is the sense of prevailing optimism. Take, Elaine Gallagher's *5AM Saint* for instance. It follows a similar tack to Hal's. Initially, we're thrust into an inauspicious cityscape where fundamentalist hate mobs run the rule over anyone they deem to be different. Again, the writing is solid, poetic, employs experimental and linear narratives, and the core message is one of tolerance and forgiveness.

Levity is provided once again by *The Glaswegian Chalk Dust Circle (or my dinner with Alan Dean Foster)*, the penultimate story by Michael Mooney. It's a fantastic exercise in cheeky, dark-caped patter while discussing the validity of the argument that Robert Heinlein wrote nothing but militaristic wank fantasies. Mooney serves up a poignant story of two boys, a closeted couple, who plan to write a science fiction story together and submit it to a competition run by the Herald – which is a lovely little nod to the GSFWC's real-life genesis. Enjoy a pint of Virus with these two acid-tongued Weegies, you won't regret it. Again, you can't miss that tone of optimism, that things usually do improve no matter how dire the circumstances appear.

Jim Steels's *The Crock of Shet* reminds us that his talents cast a wider net than his able manning of the *Interzone* reviews pile alone.

The GSFWC has provided workshops, critiques and even given young writers the opportunity to meet and mingle with their professional counterparts. It deserves to be noticed, to be loved. When you consider the calibre of writer it hones and produces, its significance cannot be denied.

In my mind, the group embodies an archetypal Scottish small-town society, one of the more successful ones at least—full of characters, united in its goals, tough as a stick of Edinburgh rock and loyal to its roots. Maybe, when we band together and formulate these utopias, there's nothing we can't achieve. Maybe we're pretty good at looking on the bright side after all.

Thirty Years of Rain is a fitting tribute to a writer's circle which has transcended its limitations and continues to exceed expectations to this day. It's rare for an anthology to offer no misfires, but after reading this book, you'll find it impossible to be a cynic.

Heart of Granite
James Barclay
Gollancz, 416 pages
Review: Ian Hunter

Apart from being the President of the British Fantasy Society, following Ramsey Campbell who held that position for decades, James Barclay is better known as the author of several fantasy series starting way back in 1999 with the *Chronicles of the Raven* trilogy, followed by other series rooted in fantasy, culminating in the recent

Elves books. Now we have *Heart of Granite*—the first in his *Blood and Fire* series. It is touted as science fiction, but is probably more science fantasy, set centuries in the future where war is being waged in a ravaged world using weapons culled from alien DNA.

Barclay has come up with the brilliant, but slightly bonkers idea of a world using DNA to create reptilian or insect-like pieces of military software—living creatures which soldiers can ride on based on creatures like geckos, iguanas or fast-moving basilisks. The Heart of Granite (or the HoG) is a leviathan creature, a behemoth and is like a living, breathing, moving aircraft carrier which houses thousands of people. People live, eat, and sleep there, and leave to fight their part of a never-ending war, and sometimes never come back again. Rather than planes flying out on missions to engage in dogfights with enemy forces, pilots fly inside drakes, or dragons.

The greatest of these pilots are those which make up the Inferno-X squadron and the best of them is Max Halloran, loved by some and hated by others, but still the pin-up boy for his side. He lives for the moment, like the rest of his crew. They might die tomorrow, or even worse, give in to the Fall, when they succumb to the mental strain of being linked to their drakes, for drake minds are too powerful and eventually human minds sink into madness.

One of his squadron is already showing those signs and will end in the area known as "Landfall" where all the "Fallen" are consigned as human vegetables. In order to save his friend, Max must journey to the secret parts of the HoG for an illegal drug which will mask and delay the effects of the Fall for a little while. But other drugs and upgrades are needed when Inferno-X are almost wiped out by an enemy squadron, upgrades which haven't been approved or tested properly. Max soon realises that they are cannon fodder, especially when an enemy leviathan is within their sights and they could deliver a killer blow to the enemy—a great result in an election year. But Max has made too many enemies and doesn't know when to shut his motor mouth or stop his fists from flying.

On trumped-up charges he ends up in Landfill and soon discovers that what he thought was the truth is far from it, but he is going to end up lost and forgotten, drugged up and tested on, unless he can do two impossible things: escape from Landfill, and then escape from the HoG, with his drake, Martha. Meanwhile, the HoG, desperately in need of some R&R, is being pushed to the limit as it pursues an equally stricken leviathan.

Heart of Granite has already been labelled "Top Gun with dragons" and likened to *Battlestar Galactica*—the gritty remake version, rather than the original— and perhaps even the gung-ho style of the *Starship Troopers* movies. Certainly, the novel is jammed packed with well-described and action-packed aerial drake-fights as well as a fair dose of political intrigue and shenanigans where no-one in authority can really be trusted. It's great fun, and a great page-turner. The book builds up to an almost *Star Wars* like climax as time and chances run out to save the HoG from enemy attack. As the novel unfolds, Max develops as a more-rounded character and Barclay leaves enough cliff-hangers and dangling threads, and enough lives in the balance to make me look forward to 2018 when the next thrilling instalment of *Blood and Fire* will appear. It can't come quickly enough.

The Hatching
Ezekiel Boone
Gollancz, 303 pages
Review: Henry Northmore

There's a rich tradition of 'when animals attack' stories in horror and sci-fi. We've been besieged by insects, rats, dogs, sharks, crabs, you name it. From classy classics such as Daphne du Maurier's *The Birds* to the splatter fiction of Shaun Hutson's *Slugs*, if it slithers, crawls or scurries it has probably risen up in defiance and attacked the human race.

Ezekiel Boone's animal of choice is spiders. Even the word is enough to evoke terror in some, sending shivers scuttling down their spine. Apparently over 35% of the population suffer from arachnophobia. And Boone

wants to dial the fear up one more notch as an ancient species of carnivorous spiders threatens to engulf the world. A black tidal wave of voracious creepy crawlies devouring everything in their path. It spreads like a living, flesh eating disease. Starting deep in the Peruvian jungle, then China becomes infested, India is next, how long before America is consumed by this eight legged tsunami?

Beyond the initial fright factor Boone turns his arthropods into a credible danger, with an intriguing life cycle, threatening to overwhelm humanity by sheer strength of numbers. How do you fight back against a swarm of bugs? Shooting bullets at a seething mass of spiders is an almost futile act.

Of course Boone isn't the first to use arachnids as his villains. There are too many monster spider movies to mention with *Tarantula* (1955), *Earth vs the Spider* (1958), *Arachnophobia* (1990) and *Eight Legged Freaks* (2002) among the minor classics across the years. However Steve Altan realised he could never beat the primal terror of *Jaws* but proved with his *Meg* series that you don't need to be the best if you can write exhilarating action sequences.

The Hatching takes too long to hit high gear and certainly isn't as engaging as some of the best in its field (James Herbert's *The Rats* is probably still the benchmark in this snapping, snarling subgenre). Boone has a predilection for clichés (including the sexy female scientist who just happens to be a world expert on spiders), he juggles too many characters, with a scant few pages devoted to each, some are invariably thinly sketched. With two more volumes planned you get the impression several are being set up

for the sequels (especially Aonghas on a remote Scottish Island and survivalists Gordo and Amy in the California desert). Inevitably as the first part of a trilogy - *Skitter* will be available in May 2017 - it ends on a cliffhanger with hints of an even bigger, nastier danger on the horizon.

Apparently the television rights have already been sold (and it would make a great TV show if someone treated the material semi-seriously rather than CBS's cheesy, trashy adaptation of James Paterson's similarly themed *Zoo*). You don't read animal amok novels expecting high art. And in that respect *The Hatching* lives up to expectations, it's no masterpiece but it's a decent page turner with enough breathless energy to drag you though the weaker sections.

Savant
Nik Abnett
Rebellion / Solaris, 356 pages
Review: Steve Ironside

Savant is set in a College—a place where the Masters (helped by their Companions and Assistants) teach their Students, while the ever-watching Service manages the schedules of them all, minute-by-minute and day-by-day. This regimen isn't just about teaching however; there's a deeper agenda to the activity of the Colleges. When the erratic behaviour of one of the Masters puts the whole system gets put at risk, Service must deal with the situation before the whole house of cards they've created comes tumbling down, with consequences that could spark an unimaginable global calamity.

As a potted synopsis, that sounded really interesting: personal drama against a backdrop of

approaching danger, set in a world of rules and authoritarian control. Just the kind of thing I was in the mood for. As always, though, the devil is in the details.

My danger sense started to tingle on page 1. I've never been a fan of inventing language just to make things sound more futuristic, and the immediate use of invented words such as "cotpro", "woolpro" and "linopro" raised flags - I wanted there to be a rationale as to why these were different from cotton, wool and lino. Maybe the College did things differently from the rest of the world; perhaps there was a reason for these different things to exist, but no real explanation was forthcoming, other than a passing reference to rationing and privilege. Whether it's Newspeak in Orwell's *1984*, or Nadsat in Burgess's *A Clockwork Orange*, the use of language permeates the setting and should inform the reader in some way; for me, there was a missed target here that turned the world into a screen upon which things were shown to me, rather than something that engaged me and drew me in.

The plot follows Metoo—an unusual woman in that she acts as both a Companion and an Assistant - and her Master Tobe, who starts to exhibit unexpected behaviour. Tobe, like all members of the College, doesn't think about the world outside of his research and teaching —as the title suggests, he's an autistic savant. With an obsessive focus on his work in addition to his mental disorder, he reacts badly to changes in his routine—much like Raymond in the movie *Rain Man*. As his new mantra that "Nothing is the same" takes root, attempts by Service to rectify the situation only make Tobe worse. The story follows the ripples of effect as they touch Metoo's life, and as events escalate further, the lives of other College personnel, and operators at Service as well.

As I progressed through the book, I felt the need to ask "why?" a lot—I wanted to understand how the world had come to be this way; why the rules of this society had come into being, and what possessed the authorities to, in essence, enslave a significant percentage of the population? Alas, I was disappointed—other than vague allusions to a global catastrophe that start to surface later in the book, the world outside of the College and Service remains mostly unexplored. While this can be used to good effect in a story—take the movie *Cube* as a terrific example—it only really works if the world outside the story is either completely irrelevant, or is a central part of the book's mystery and is intended to force the reader to imagine. In *Savant*, the world lies somewhere in-between—the external environment and its pressures directly affect the decisions that Service makes. However, because I couldn't see that bigger picture, none of these choices felt particularly urgent, or made me sympathetic to either the characters, or the pressures that they are under. The glimpses that were handed out just served to make me want to know why, as opposed to inviting me to imagine what could actually be going on.

Despite these misgivings, I did find the book to be an easy read—the story rattles along at a comfortable pace, and beyond the College environment there are a couple of characters that I did find very engaging.

It's a readable story that I finished in a couple of sittings. However, it's not a book that I would return to again. *Savant* is ultimately emotionally flat and unsatisfying. That's a shame, because I suspect that outside of the College, there is a fascinating world waiting to be revealed.

Empire Games
Charles Stross
Tor, 316 pages
Review: Noel Chidwick

Empire Games continues the Merchant Princes series, which we left in 2010 with the *Trade of Queens*.

The Merchant Princes is an alternative Earth saga, featuring the Clan, who world-walk between their own timeline still stuck in the Middle Ages and 'our' timeline. They trade between the two lines to make their fortune, where trade is, as Stross describes it, "paperwork-free shipping." Drugs trafficking is their currency: the obvious choice when you can flick from one world to another in the blink of an eye.

The upshot is knights with machine guns.

If you haven't read the Merchant Princes books, off you pop. They're a riveting read and you'll be turning pages so fast you'll risk finger blisters.

The bulk of *Empire Games* is set in 2020, with a President Rumsfeld in the big chair. We follow in the footsteps of Rita, who is the daughter of Miriam, the protagonist of the original series. Rita is adopted, and initially is unaware of the identity of her "DNA Donors", just as her mother was before her at the start of the original series.

We're quickly drawn into a shadowy world where the USA is developing a defence program to protect itself, as it sees, from the terrorism of the Clan, using technology and not-so-nice means to create ways to world-hop with big machinery and weapons of war.

Meanwhile, the Clan, after having to move to a third timeline are also building up their power in a once vaguely Victorian timeline.

Miriam seems to have a lot of say, and this timeline quickly develops technologies to help better the lives of the Clan and its host world, and to protect itself against the looming US threat.

Rita is the pivot in this tale, as she is trained and persuaded to help in the US's desire for intelligence on the whereabouts of the Clan, and ways to destroy it.

The section of Rita's training is the one area where Stross strays to cliché a tad, and you can almost hear the pulsing music-backed montage in the film version, but in this case it serves as a vehicle for Rita to begin to question herself and ask what the heck is really going on.

Stross is a master of world weaving and narrative time hopping. To reach 2020 we leapfrog from the present day, skipping across timelines as we go. As we jump around we neatly revisit the backstory of the previous series, popping in useful reminders as we go. This viewpoint movement helps build the tension and at the same time helps grow that sense of unease. I read this book on a short visit to Gothenburg; finding myself in a country with a language I had no handle on (French or Spanish yes, Swedish—not a chance), probably enhanced that feeling of discombobulation.

Stross is good at writing strong female characters, especially in his recent books, and Empire Games is no different. Rita's passage from ignorance to awareness, and eventually to a real sense of what's she getting into is handled believably. Miriam meanwhile, in her timeline is strong-willed and determined, but with a sense of what is right. Her self-doubt, however, acts as a check and balance for her actions. Rita's uncle plays a large role in the backroom of the story; an immigrant to the US from a pre-wall East Germany.

From time to time Stross takes a wander off the path of the furiously building story to enjoy his many worlds and to give us tantalising glimpses of ideas he's brewing. There's a world with a hole in it that really does need looking into; no doubt the rest of the series will give Stross the space to explore that and other worlds he's hinted at. Watch those blistering fingers as you turn the pages. Empire Games is fast-paced, intricate and thoroughly captivating. I look forward to reading the rest of the series.

Multiverse
Russell Jones

What better way to forget the past than to imagine the future? The poems in this issue of *Shoreline of Infinity* explore (amongst other things) memory, and a desire to build, reconstruct or break links with the past.

Grahaeme Barrasford Young kicks us off with "War species", in which the speaker asks "what makes breakers of worlds believe / their galaxy will want them near". A haunting prediction for human-kind's future relationship with the universe and the species within it, perhaps? This poem can't help but resonate with anyone who's concerned with current political and ecological struggles, ending with an approaching (human) darkness: "new neighbours ask // why black holes suddenly seem so bright".

"the inevitable victory of attraction" also deals with human (im)perception and (lack of) self awareness, asking, "how can we watch ourselves // individually if rods and stems / are made of what they see", and implies that adaptation is key to our progress: "unusually, particles suggest / imbalanced elements will combine". Here, then, blindly longing for the status quo of the past is what leads us to doom. Make of that what you will, British and American politicians!

J.S. Watt's "Returnings" offers a more personal slant on the nature and purpose of memory. The speaker attempts to compromise their two distinct emotions: belonging to the past is balanced against the excitement and trepidation of the future. This can be read as a poem about love, or a dismantled relationship, but also about the way we balance our sense of self with our personal history and desire to evolve as individuals.

"Starscape" considers the importance of personal reflection and humanity within art: "My poetry is starscapes, black expanse of emptiness … All the same. / Infinity is relentless without / life's gravity to anchor it." Yet the individual also seems lost amongst the vastness and emptiness of a universe which doesn't speak back: "The universal ellipse reflects only itself". The devil's in the detail, then. What is life without those specific moments of joy? Vast emptiness which cannot be tamed or understood.

Like us, our ancestors have looked on the stars and wondered. Those distant flickering lights link us to that past, but they also remind us of our potential futures: as individuals, members of a nation and a species. These poems use the metaphors of space to remind us that self-reflection is vital to our progress and continued survival, or damnation.

War species

when we have finished with our system
do you think we can wander freely

what makes breakers of worlds believe
their galaxy will want them near

where, in that case, will be an awful way
very few embarking will survive

who, entering occupied space
will have to make their choice

which we ancestors can only hope
does not make new neighbours ask

why black holes suddenly seem bright
through the darkness just arrived.

Grahaeme Barrasford Young

Erstwhile editor, publisher and printer, **Grahaeme Barrasford Young** returned
to serious writing at the turn of the century. He is widely published. His collection,
Routes of Uncertainty (Original Plus), appeared in 2014.

the inevitable victory of attraction

particularly, atoms reproduce
Seurat on a smaller larger scale

spectacularly, they compose
an observed universe that

lullingly, feels like home
whatever answer we impose

conversely, being atoms
how can we watch ourselves

individually if rods and stems
are made of what they see

painfully obscuring dot on dot
and therefore missing other dots

universally massing our horizons
with spaces galaxies can slip between

selfishly pretending autonomy
from orbiting others when

unusually, particles suggest
imbalanced elements will combine

improbably to ambivalent nuclei
when time sucks them back

inevitably to that long ago future point
we do not want to remember

Grahaeme Barrasford Young

Returnings

The moon rose dark tonight. It is time to go back,
to the beginnings, the old ways, the old gods.
Your light has begun to blind me.
I lost myself for a lifetime
in its electric brightness, its ecstatic neon glance,
but now I know that all it was
was that I could not see to see.
The moon still has a daughter, even across the ocean,
and though her light is dimmed
by the passing of your glory
her darkness is generous and all embracing.
It will welcome me again.

Do not underestimate my grief. I mourn your loss,
the absence of your brightness, the light in the blue
teaching me the beauty of drowning,
but it is time to drown out of my own depth,
in the black moon-dragged waters of my own kind.
My history is trying to get back to me.
I gave you my dull past
and you illuminated possibilities
that spun the world one hundred and eighty degrees,
revealing coloured paths we ran down
skin in soul and others more gently tinted
for walking through together, though we never did.

Habit still places my feet on your bright yellow road.
I am not yet ready for the wilderness of this next rotation,
the circling of the eagle over the corpse of the bear.
I am not a nomad, a dreamer of hopeless dreams.
If I hold my hope in empty hands, I do so knowingly
to display my loss. I will not blame you
for what you cannot do.
Old imperatives ache darkly along my bones.
The eagle and the bear will never dance together
under an orange sun
but they can lie down together in the dark and wait to die.
Black is the ultimate equalizer.

The moon has made the transition already:
her silver tarnished to dark.
It will be my turn soon: a returning,
back to the night where I am known
where there is no one and nothing else to know.
Let me say goodbye in the shadow of your radiance.
Farewell draws down despair more slowly if you remain,
illuminating for a brief while longer my first steps
off our path into the no woman's land that waits
before the moon's true salt engulfs me entirely.
Her tides, sacred waters, will wash me free of your stain,
purifying me of me before I am come again home.

J.S. Watts

Starscape

If I were writing then
I'd take my stylus, pencil, e-vice
to a woodland clearing, up
where the hills bolstered me like pillows.
I'd lie down on my back
wondering at the distant stars
through the lens of the encircling trees
and my poetry would be landscape,
hills, rivers, trees and soil.
The places where our roots lie buried.

Out here my roots float free,
snaking through the cosmos in search
of a new Eden to anchor them
but finding only more space.
My poetry is starscapes,
black expanse of emptiness
with pin pricks of raw perfection.
All different. All the same.
Infinity is relentless without
life's gravity to anchor it.

There is no love amongst the stars,
just a limitless absence of hope.
No land where I can sink my feet.
Planets are pretty marbles,
stars, cold exploding beauty,
the crystal sphere of each black hole,
a marvel of endless consumption.
This ship's reinforced stellar hull,
as thin as bubbles compared
to the starscape it drifts aimlessly through.

The universal ellipse reflects only itself,
endlessly repeating the extremism of creation,
echoes of a promise kept once
in the past and maybe again, eons beyond this future.
My mind's eye, the only lens through which
I can wonder distantly at our lost frail world.
The unseen curves of space
circle my fading muse
like the starving dog packs
circled the last prey on Earth.

J.S. Watts

J.S. Watts is a UK writer with five books to her name: three of poetry, *Cats and Other Myths*, *Songs of Steelyard Sue* and *Years Ago You Coloured Me* (published by Lapwing Publications) and two novels, *A Darker Moon* and *Witchlight* (published by Vagabondage Press). Her website is: www.jswatts.co.uk

---

Parabolic Puzzles
Paul Holmes

Crossing the Bridge

In the bleak midwinter, on their way to the Annual Jazz Club Christmas Bash, four band members carrying their instruments came to a rickety old bridge bearing the sign

"Warning – Rickety Bridge – only two people to cross at any one time".

This was particularly sage advice as there was a thin covering of snow.

Art, carrying his flute, was the quickest and could cross the bridge in two minutes, whereas Bennie, carrying his rather valuable clarinet which would never leave his side, was a little more cautious, and would only cross in three minutes.

Charlie, carrying a saxophone but nursing an injured knee, could only hobble across in eight minutes, whereas Duke, lugging a double bass, could only make the crossing in ten minutes.

To complicate matters, they only had one lantern between them, which was vital as it was dark and the bridge had slats missing.

How quickly could they make the crossing?

The Return Crossing

On their way home, they now have Ella, the singer, returning with them. She is rather elderly now and will take 12 minutes to cross the bridge. She knows this because she timed herself just a few minutes before her four colleagues made their original crossing. Cursing the fact that someone built the jazz club on the wrong side of the ravine, they pause at the entrance to the bridge and try to work out how long it will take to cross.

What is the shortest time it takes our five musicians to cross the rickety bridge?

Send your answer to us via our website Contact Form. If you are correct, your name will be dropped into a hat. A copy of Duncan Lunan's book The Elements of Time *will be sent to the lucky name pulled out of said hat.*

Paul's latest collection of Puzzles, *The Galactic Festival* has just been published by Shoreline of Infinity Publications. Available from www.shorelineofinfinity.com or from your favourite bookshop.

9 780099 344136